FRIDAY THE SIXTEENTH

FRIDAY
THE
SIXTEENTH

PETER COOMBS

Matador
9 Priory Business Park,
Wistow Road, Kibworth Beauchamp,
Leicestershire. LE8 0RX
Tel: 0116 279 2299
Email: books@troubador.co.uk
Web: www.troubador.co.uk/matador
Twitter: @matadorbooks

ISBN 978 1800463 905

British Library Cataloguing in Publication Data.
A catalogue record for this book is available from the British Library.

Printed and bound in Great Britain by 4edge Limited
Typeset in 11pt Baskerville by Troubador Publishing Ltd, Leicester, UK

Matador is an imprint of Troubador Publishing Ltd

This book is dedicated to Liz.
Thank you for always being there.

ONE

Friday the sixteenth. Two days before Sunday the eighteenth. He didn't know it yet, but it would all start on Sunday and his life would never be the same again.

He was a big man. Not big as in fat, but big as in imposing; he had a definite presence. The expression 'once seen, never forgotten' could have been written about Andrew Packford. Years of manual work had ensured that he was in good shape. He had no need to visit a gym but he did twice a week, simply because he liked it. He liked the feeling of pushing himself, both mentally and physically. For a big man, he moved around the small apartment with a cat-like grace. Every movement, every action, no matter how insignificant or how ordinary, was carried out in a controlled way. The way he now controlled his life.

Every day was different, with a different routine. Today was Friday. He liked Fridays.

He washed and shaved as usual. He prepared his usual breakfast, orange juice, toast and instant coffee, no sugar. He liked to take his time over it. He had no reason to rush. There was plenty of time for what he had to do.

Now every day presented new challenges, but he would meet them head-on. In his own controlled way. On his terms. After all those years of doing what he was told. Doing what everyone wanted; everyone except him. Now he was making his own decisions; sink or swim, rise or fall, famine or feast. Whichever way you cut it, it was going to be on his back, and ultimately the benefits would be in his pocket and in his peace of mind. No more orders from some anonymous voice on the end of a telephone.

He couldn't help himself, every day he compared his new life to the old one. In the beginning it had been all he had ever wanted, but times change. Most people have a dream. Sometimes that dream stays with them all their life, sometimes the dream turns into a nightmare. Andy's dream turned into his nightmare.

He had always wanted to be his own person, to travel his own highway, quite literally in his case.

On reflection, it wasn't all bad. At first life had been good. It had been a challenge that he was prepared to meet. It was all he ever wanted, to be free to be his own man. Instead of the knight in shining armour, he realised too late that he was more like the whipping boy.

As a twenty-one-year-old, he had realised his boyhood ambition, a dream come true. Following in his father's footsteps, he qualified as a lorry driver. Not just any lorry, from now on, he would be driving forty-ton articulated monsters. For a while he was more than content travelling the length and breadth of Britain carrying everything from fruit and vegetables to machine parts. He had done it all with a smile. Well, mostly with a smile. From massive industrial complexes to tiny back street workshops, he'd been to them all. Like most things in life, it didn't last forever. It didn't take too long for the sugar coating to wear off.

The long days and the nights trying to sleep parked up in a noisy lay-by. The rush to get home before he ran out of hours or risked another sleepless night in a lorry cab. The arguments with his wife, the missed dinner dates and the eventual, inevitable separation. Then the green warriors appeared on the scene. *Ban all lorries from the motorways. Make them all travel at night. Put the freight on the railways. Yeah, yeah. We don't want nasty, big lorries.* Mostly the voices of the upmarket wives. The wives of business professionals. The voice of middle England, who should know better. The very same wives who go into a hissy fit if the supermarket runs out of fresh salmon or asparagus. How do they think this stuff gets there? The same wives who park on double yellows because they can't reverse their Mini into a parking bay. The same wives who expect lorry drivers to disappear into a space that doesn't exist.

As he thought about his previous life, he had no way of knowing how one particular upmarket wife would be the catalyst that would start events that would spiral out of control.

If there is one thing that driving a truck does, it gives you time to think. Time to think about what you would be doing if you weren't stuck on the M25 or at junction 23 of the M1, or anywhere else, because eventually every traffic jam is the same. All that changes is the vehicle next to you. A car full of kids bored out of their minds until a friendly truck driver pulled faces at them, making them forget about the Nintendo or the TV screen. Young faces covered in chocolate that returned toothy grins until their parents realised they were being entertained by a nasty lorry driver! The irony wasn't lost on Andy. While he was trying to make his contribution to British industry, these kids were growing up. In a few years they would be sitting in a car next to him, frantically looking at their watch or talking on their phone, trying to explain why they were going to be late for that important appointment. Some of those freckled, smiling kids would become suits. Suits are always in a hurry, wanting to be somewhere else half an hour ago.

Andy had put those years and wasted hours in traffic jams to good use. He'd had plenty of time to think. He knew what he wanted to do, and he knew darn well what he didn't want to do. He didn't want to take any more crap from a suit in an office. A suit who had never got their hands dirty, never sweated loading and unloading a lorry, or used their charm and tact to ensure that some bad-tempered warehouse foreman would see that he was loaded and on his way before his hours ran out. Yes, he had tact and determination in bucketloads.

He also had a passion. In fact, he had two. He had a passion for wheels. In his younger days it was bicycle wheels. As a schoolboy he did whatever he could to make money. Odd jobs at home and for neighbours, anything to make a few coppers. An eye for a profit that would pay dividends in later life. He had managed to save enough to buy his first dream. A hand-built Italian Colnago racing bicycle. The same cycle he had seen his heroes ride in the Tour de France. Good enough to help him win his cycle club's junior championship. He still kept the medal where he could look at it, and those visits to the gym kept his body in good shape. Maybe not racing fit, but still pretty good. After the Colnago it was motorbikes; Kawasaki, a spluttering little 125, which was quickly followed by the powerful 750 that he still kept in his garage. A succession of cars followed. Whilst his heart said to buy an exciting sports car, his pocket said to buy something sensible, and for the time being he was happy with his elderly BMW estate.

His other passion was slightly older. Antiques.

Any antiques. Just the thought of buying something old, anything, and knowing that in a previous life somebody had used and cherished it. It didn't matter if it was a silver watch chain or a rusty corkscrew. Someone had walked to a shop and chosen it. No cars or buses in the nineteenth century. Possibly a horse, but more likely they walked, the thought of what they might buy filling their mind as they travelled and the satisfaction with the purchase as they returned home. How different is that to our modern, throwaway, don't care world?

A watch chain that has hung in a waistcoat pocket day after day. How many times has it been pulled in and out? How many times has it been sat on the dressing table whilst the owner slept or made love? How many family dinners has the host used the corkscrew? How many happy and sad occasions had the owner taken its simple mechanics for granted? Andy revelled in the mysteries and found a fulfilling satisfaction in the thought that simple items can transcend generations and still give immense pleasure. Antiques gave Andy a lot more than pleasure; they also gave him a good living. No more long hours driving, no more sleeping in a lorry cab, no more grief from irate storemen. For the past three years, life had been very good indeed.

He couldn't help but think what might have been. He blamed the long hours away from home for the breakup of his marriage. That and the fact that he and Sarah seemed unable to produce the much longed for child. He dismissed the thought as he left home and got into the BMW.

TWO

Fifty miles to the north, a group of dedicated men were readying themselves for a long weekend. They had arrived early to open up. Telcote Manor was a large, sprawling Victorian manor house, once owned by the local vicar. The long gravel drive curved slightly to reveal the magnificence of the house. Originally built in the early nineteenth century, it was obvious that the current owner had spared neither time nor money to bring it back to its present spectacular condition. To the rear were several large barns originally they had housed the horses and riding buggies, now they provided shelter to a different kind of power. One of the men opened and secured the large doors and switched on the lights. They carefully checked that everything was as they had left it. Then they settled into a well-practiced routine.

They started with the numerous boxes, all different sizes, all numbered, followed by specialised racks and hoists. They all had to be loaded into their own individual place in the lorry. To Howard Fryer it was just another weekend, the same as every other weekend for as long as he could remember. Except that in the early days, men like him relied on their instincts, their hearing, even their sense of smell; nowadays, they relied on computer screens and readouts. So, they loaded banks of computers into the lorry. When everything was securely fastened away, they started the real work of the day. They slowly and carefully slid the tailored dust sheets from the car. Howard opened the doors and bonnet and began his meticulous inspection.

One of the team joked, "He knows more about that car then he does about his missus."

Some of them laughed. Howard Fryer didn't.

They all knew that this final inspection was just a formality. Howard had checked and double-checked everything yesterday before putting his baby to bed. They also knew that it was his obsession with detail that made him the best mechanic in the world of historic sports car racing. Every one of them, from his long-time assistant to the young gofer, was proud to be part of the team. A race-winning team. Even years ago, before every team in the paddock relied on data from a laptop, they were the crew behind most of the race-winning drivers. When Howard was satisfied that everything was as it should be, he eased himself into the driving seat and carefully pressed the starter button.

For a few seconds they all held their breath. Then they covered their ears as seven litres of Detroit V8 burst into life, sucking fuel through the Holley carburettors at a rate that only a very rich man would consider acceptable, drowning out any other noise on that March morning. Carefully, he eased the Ford Mustang out of the workshop and onto the hydraulic lift on the back of the lorry. Slowly and precisely, the lift was raised, and in time the car was safely secured inside the belly of the lorry.

THREE

Like most auction houses, Miller and Jackman Fine Arts Ltd make their money by selling people's unwanted possessions. In the main, they are unwanted because the owner is dead. Not a very comforting thought that when you die, dozens of grubby hands are going to rifle through your belongings. But that's how it is. Sometimes the proceeds pay the inheritance tax bill, sometimes they pay for the nursing care. But one thing is sure: when you are dead, you can't take them with you.

Antique sales vary. Auctioneers can only sell what they are given. There are times when, inconveniently, nobody has died. Rather than have an empty saleroom, they usually encourage their favourite dealers to consign a few bits and bobs, generally the overpriced rubbish they can't sell in their shops or on their stalls. Most dealers are so keen to offload their old stock that, in their haste, they forget to take off the price label or stock code. Even if they take these off, experienced dealers like Andy can spot this unwanted stock a mile away and keep well clear. Nobody wants to try to sell someone else's unsold leftovers.

"New to the trade" is the expression, and every dealer wants stock that is "new to the trade".

This week's sale looked promising. Andy had checked out the auction catalogue online and had already made a list of the lots he was keen to buy. Most dealers try to specialise in certain areas of antiques. There are good reasons for doing this. Firstly, if you learn your craft, you will become something of an expert in that particular field, something that your customers will find comforting and reassuring. Secondly, you will know exactly how much you can afford to pay for a particular piece because you know how much you sold the last one for.

Andrew Packford specialised in sewing implements. Anything from a thimble to a sewing workbox. It might be considered a strange speciality for a large, imposing man, someone you would class as a man's man. But, as with all his decisions, there was sound reasoning behind it. Most of the items were quite small; thimbles, pincushions, scissors, needle boxes were all tiny. They didn't take up much room. When they were packed away they easily fitted into the back of his car, which made life very easy when travelling to the various markets and antique centres around the country. More importantly, they would easily fit into the pocket or handbag of the ladies who formed the majority of his customers. Even the larger sewing worktables would easily fit into the boot of any small hatchback.

Selling these small items was very lucrative, the more desirable thimbles selling for forty or fifty pounds, and pincushions up to a couple of hundred pounds. As with his previous career, Andy always thought things through, always covered all the bases and always knew what his next move would be.

"Good morning, ladies and gentlemen, it's ten o'clock, time to start today's sale."

FOUR

Already two hours late to start his shift, Graham Jones knew he was in for another rollicking. He wasn't sure how much more of this his boss would stand for before he was shown the door. In fact, knowing his boss, it wasn't so much a case of being shown the door, more a case of being kicked through it. He knew that one way or another he would have to make up for lost time. He had a choice, skip tea and lunch breaks or cut corners to boost production. Today he might have to do both. Nothing unusual.

His life was rubbish at the moment and losing his job would be the last straw.

The very last straw.

Since he and Allison had moved into their new home with daughter Jessica, their lives had hit rock bottom. They were expecting a new start. A new house, a bright new beginning. That is what they had been promised. After years of living in damp substandard houses, the local authorities had eventually allocated them a new home on a brand-new estate. They had hoped for a new beginning but quickly found that things were getting worse, much worse. Why did these things always happen to them? Why is it that when you are down, everything bad happens to you? The harder you try to dig yourself out of a hole, the more you slide back down. Why don't the smiling-faced celebrities in the papers get the same crap deal?

Hollybush Close was in the far corner of a modern housing development. Large, impressive five bedroom houses flanked the entrance to the estate, with neatly tended gardens and a Volvo or Mercedes in the drive. The head of the household working in middle management. All typical 2.4 family stuff. As you drove through the estate, the road dipped away slightly and the apparent quality of the homes followed suit. By the time you got to Hollybush Close, tucked away out of sight, the detached houses had given way to rows of small terraces. Instead of smart Mercedes in the drive, there were discarded child's toys and bicycles. As with all modern estates, this was the area given over to affordable housing, the expression used by the government and local councils to imply that people on lesser incomes can actually afford to buy a house. In reality, the houses were rented from either a private landlord or from a housing association. The opportunity to own their own house would still be a distant dream for most of the occupants.

Graham, Allison and baby Jessica fitted the profile perfectly. Loving, caring parents working as hard as they knew how, but sadly always slipping backwards and nobody cared. Not many people visited the far corner of the estate.

FIVE

Victor Manning eased himself into his leather chair and looked around his office. On the wall behind his desk was his favourite photograph. Not surprisingly, it was a picture of Victor Manning. In fact, the walls were covered with pictures of Victor Manning.

Some of them were of him and his family, taken in the grounds of Telcote Manor but mostly they were of him and his Ford Mustang. Him and the Mustang at Donington Park. Him and the Mustang at Zandvoort. In fact, him and the Mustang at just about every racing circuit. For a man who had made millions of pounds from the thousands of houses he had built, there was surprisingly little photographic evidence of his work, only of the rewards.

He didn't intend to do much work in the office today, he never did on Fridays. He would leave about lunchtime and drive the thirty-odd miles to Donington Park. He had heard nothing from Howard Fryer. He knew that in this case, no news was definitely good news. From past experience, he knew better than to call him. A distracting ring on a mobile phone would prompt a foul-mouthed rant from Fryer.

Manning was accustomed to getting his own way, accustomed to upsetting people, but he was also used to using people. He wasn't using Fryer and his men; he was depending on them.

When Howard was ready, he would phone. There was very little for Manning to do in the office today. There never was. In the early days of Viman Developments he had done it all, but now he had people and he had money. He knew full well that money had bought him respectability and his money paid their wages, so he had no need to do it all.

Angela was in her late thirties. Young enough to still be very attractive and desirable, and certainly old enough to know it. She entered his office without knocking; she didn't have to. Everyone else was expected to knock, and everyone else knew that if she wasn't at her desk, they were expected to knock and wait.

In the seven years she had worked as his P. A. they had never been caught in the act, so to speak but it was no secret that things went on in his office. Things were not going to be going on today, not on a Friday. He would need all his concentration for the coming weekend. Then if it was a good weekend, there would be plenty of time for things.

Although his mind was elsewhere, it didn't stop him casting an eye over her ample cleavage as she bent over to present the day's letters for signing, or stop him watching her well-rounded bottom as she turned to leave. Her perfume hung in the air long after she had left the room. He wondered if it was perfume that he had bought. Maybe he had, maybe her husband had, maybe she had another admirer. Maybe she had, he didn't care.

So long as what he wanted was available when he wanted it, he didn't care.

SIX

At Holdstock Quarry, Graham didn't want to stay longer to make up for his late start. God knows he was tired enough without having to work more hours. Instead of working late, he would try to get his production quota completed the best way he knew. If need be he would cut corners but only when no one was looking.

As he operated the ancient, gigantic mechanical shovel, his mind was not really on the job. Instead, he wondered how Allison had got on at the doctors. Since moving into Hollybush Close, baby Jessica had not stopped crying. He and Alison both suspected that she had caught a virus or a bug of some sort. Three times they had taken her to the doctor, only to be told that it was nothing serious. Yet still she cried all night and most of the day. As he operated the shovel, he prayed that the doctor would listen to reason and refer his Angel to the hospital so that she might at last get some proper attention.

Everyone at Holdstock knew the shovel was an antique, a relic that should have been replaced years ago. At the very least, it should have had regular, documented servicing, properly carried out and properly entered into the service book. Instead, they had used an unqualified mechanic with no experience of the equipment. Someone who was prepared to apply a little oil here and there, while the worn-out internal workings went unchecked and unattended. The management was happy to falsify the service log, anything to save a few pounds. Anything to make more money.

Graham, like everyone else at the quarry, knew what was going on but was powerless to stop it. If they complained too much, they were "up the road" as the boss so succinctly put it. If they shopped him to the health and safety inspector, the quarry would in all probability be shut down. Either way, they were up the road.

The bucket jammed for the third time that morning. Instead of dropping two tons of gravel into the waiting tipper, it hovered over the open lorry. Graham left the cab of the mechanical shovel and climbed down. The usual procedure was to climb onto the lorry and give the stubborn bucket a few hefty swings with a spade. Not very technical and not particularly safe, but it had been effective for as long as Graham could remember. And it was quick.

SEVEN

Andy found himself a quiet corner in Miller and Jackman's saleroom. He had bought a cup of coffee from the adjacent tea stall and he waited for the auctioneer to reach the lots that he would bid on.

Antique auctions vary in the order the various items are sold. Some auction houses, for instance, start with china and glass, carry through to fine jewellery and similar items, and finish with the furniture. Others will mix all the different items together, so in the catalogue an antique diamond ring could preceded by a longcase clock and followed by an old bicycle. Luckily, Miller and Jackman sold their antiques in order, so when the auctioneer finally reached the ten or twelve lots Andy was after he could hopefully buy what he wanted and then go home. He was assuming that he was not going to be outbid.

Like any sensible dealer, he always set himself a maximum figure that he was prepared to pay for a given item. He knew only too well that a lot of dealers suffer from nameitis. That is, the love of hearing their name called out as the successful bidder. In the antiques business, it is a very prevalent disease.

The desire to hear your name seems to outweigh the need to trade profitably. Many sufferers of this disease also suffer from the doctor's wife syndrome.

Rather unfairly, that is the term many experienced dealers give to the ladies who are given a few thousand pounds by their well-off partners to go and play at "antique dealers". Of course, not all the well-off partners are doctors, but they are mostly professional men, possibly accountants or architects. The one thing they have in common is that they congratulate their wives on the number of purchases made at the saleroom. After all, it is not as if they need to make a profit, not like a real dealer.

The first of Andy's lots was a group of Charles Horner silver thimbles. Charles Horner being the important name in early twentieth century silverware. The bids quickly rose to Andy's maximum. He knew from past mistakes that if he bid any higher, he would not make a profit and, more importantly, he would tie up his capital without much chance of getting a sale. So, with a great deal of reluctance, he shook his head when the auctioneer looked in his direction.

The bidding war continued between two ladies. The lot was finally knocked down to Mrs Harrison. It was obviously Mrs. Harrison's day as she managed to buy most of the lots that Andy had set his mind on. With only one more item to bid on, a small late Victorian sewing table in very poor condition, Andy felt confident that Mrs Harrison would not want to fix the damaged veneer and broken legs. He turned his head to her and looked at her long, elegant fingers and her beautifully manicured nails.

There was no way these hands were going to cut and fit fine veneer or go anywhere near a glue pot. Possibly a bone china coffee cup in some chic little café along with the other doctor's wives but definitely nowhere near a glue pot.

So. he readied himself to try and salvage something from an otherwise wasted day.

Optimistically, the auctioneer tried to open the bidding at one hundred pounds.

"A hundred pounds to start, surely…Fifty then…I'm bid a disappointing twenty…Any further bids?"

A few more half-hearted bids and it was finally knocked down to Andy for thirty-two pounds plus buyer's commission. Not a brilliant day, but at least there would be a profit at the end of it. With a day working on the little table, he thought he could probably sell it for two hundred and fifty pounds. Well, maybe two hundred after a little haggling.

Still not too bad for a day's work. Andy joined the queue outside the cashier's office, ready to pay for his one lot. A few places in front of him Mrs, Harrison was also waiting to pay. She was a very striking lady, probably in her early forties, tall, slim, with a nice figure. Andy formed a picture in his mind of her and her husband smiling for the camera on the society pages of the local paper.

He collected his sewing table, together with all the little chips and pieces that had fallen off thanks to the constant handling the table had received during the viewing period and carefully carried it out to his old BMW estate in the car park.

As was usual on sale days, the car park was jammed solid. It reminded Andy of his lorry driving days. Everyone wanted to be as close as possible to the entrance and everyone was in a bigger hurry than the next person. The driver of a scruffy Ford Transit had parked directly in front of the BMW and was in the process of loading the various lots he had bought at the auction. Rather than cause an argument by asking him to move, Andy reckoned that he wouldn't be too much longer. As he waited, he thought about the auction lots that he had been outbid on.

Darn it! He was an expert in his field. If Mrs. Society page Harrison was prepared to pay more than him for the Charles Horner thimbles and all the other items, she must know something that he didn't or maybe she was just a chancer who didn't need to make a profit. He was still smarting over the situation when the lady in question walked across in front of him and went to a small, brightly painted van. It was one of those dainty little vans that are favoured by florists or dog groomers. On the side, in large letters, was *Marie-Ann Antiques*.

Andy tried not to think about the auction as he drove home. The Friday afternoon traffic was heavier and slower than normal, which didn't improve his frustration. As he approached M1 junction 23A, the queue of vehicles ground to a halt. In front of him he could see several large lorries, some towing trailers, all emblazoned with motor racing advertisements and sponsors. He reasoned they were making their way to the nearby Donington Park race circuit. Then he remembered that this weekend, Donington was hosting the first round of the International Historic Touring Car championship. Andy cheered himself up with the thought that on Sunday, he would take a day off from antiques and go to watch the motor racing. Feeling slightly happier with himself, he didn't notice the ambulance travelling in the other direction.

EIGHT

The emergency siren was wailing fit to waken the dead. Everyone at the quarry knew what it meant. In the back of the tipper lorry, the driver was frantically clawing at the heap of gravel with his bare hands. As he thrust his hands in and out of the sliding, moving mass, the blood dripped from his fingertips and tears rolled down his unshaven cheeks.

Soon he was joined by others with shovels and spades.

Standing alone to the rear of the lorry, George Ashton was struggling to make himself heard.

"As manager of this quarry, I am ordering you men to maintain health and safety standards and wear high-vis jackets and hard hats."

No one listened, no one looked up, no one stopped digging.

"We will be crucified by the health and safety inspector. You must wear the right gear." He protested.

"It's a bit bloody late for that," was the breathless reply from somewhere inside the lorry.

To those that were digging, it seemed like hours. In reality, it probably took no more than ten or twelve minutes to uncover Graham Jones' body. His face was covered in blood, which had congealed with the sand and gravel to form a grotesque mask. His head and shoulders had taken the full force of the falling contents of the jammed excavator bucket, all two tons of it. His workmates gently cleaned the muck and grime from his face and carefully, very carefully, laid his lifeless body on the ground.

Even over the quarry emergency siren, they could hear the sound of the approaching ambulance. Several waving arms directed it as close as they could to the scene of the accident.

Ashton ran to the ambulance.

"Health and safety are our main priorities here. I don't know how an accident like this could happen, our workmen always wear full safety equipment, these rescuers have only just taken off their jackets and helmets."

The paramedics gently but firmly pushed him to one side.

Ashton carried on regardless. "We have an excellent safety record here at Holdstock. I'm always instructing the men to do things properly and report anything they think might need attention."

The ambulance crew went through their well-practised routine, oblivious to George Ashton's pathetic lies.

"There is a pulse. It's not much, but it is there."

With the care and precision that only comes with years of training and dedication, Graham's body was stretchered into the ambulance and when they were ready, they quickly departed for the hospital.

Harry Thornton had been a tipper driver for more than ten years. For most of those years, he had been collecting gravel from various quarries, including Holdstock, so he knew how a safe quarry should be managed, and he knew that Holdstock was anything but a safe quarry. Strangely, although he had nothing good to say about the management, he always got on well with the workmen, and particularly Graham.

They had shared the odd tea break, when Graham had excitedly told him about the new house he and Allison were moving into and later, he had heard Graham's despair that their baby was not well.

To those people who saw him driving his truck, Harry was a typical old-school lorry driver. Half-smoked roll-up between his lips, usually unshaven, tattoos on his muscular arms. The sort of man you don't really want to upset. The sort of man you would rather not sit close to in the pub. That was on the outside. On the inside, he was a family man, he liked to talk about his own kids and he liked to hear about other people's. It always upset him to hear Graham speak about his sick daughter. He knew that Graham was a decent chap trying to make a decent life for himself and his family, and Harry knew he was fighting a losing battle.

Harry knew all about the excavator bucket seizing up every now and then and he knew how they would swing at it with the spade. How many times had he told Graham to make sure that the manager got it fixed, and how many times had Graham said that the manager didn't want to know? Well, he knew now.

As the ambulance turned out of the site to begin the fifteen-mile journey to the hospital, it nearly collided with the police car that was driving in. Obviously the police had been alerted by the emergency call centre. George Ashton was running as fast as his bloated legs would allow, not to escape from the scene of the tragedy but in a vain attempt to get the exhausted rescuers into a coherent, manageable group.

Sergeant John Grove had been a police officer for eighteen years. There was very little that he hadn't either seen or had to sort out. As he opened the door of his patrol car and straightened his six feet two inches tall frame his very presence left nobody in any doubt. Now he was in charge of this situation.

"Can the person in charge of this quarry please make themselves known?"

"Yes, Officer, that would be me. I'm George Ashton, the quarry manager. Any of these men here will tell you that this is one of the safest quarries in the country. I ensure that all the equipment is of the highest possible standard, but unfortunately the injured employee was always ignoring the safety procedures behind my—"

Before he could finish the sentence, Harry pushed his way through the group of men who were now forming a slowly tightening circle around the increasingly agitated manager.

"Officer, I swear to God that if you don't take this lying, swindling bastard into custody, I will personally make sure that he spends the rest of his miserable life in a wheelchair, I saw first-hand what happened today and every time I drive to this shithole of a quarry I see the total disregard of any safety procedures. I see the worn-out machinery that he refuses to replace and the appalling conditions that his men are forced to work under. The injured man was a young guy trying to make a life for himself and his family. If he dies, it will be the fault of this miserable cretin."

The circle of men cheered as they edged still closer. Grove

realised he was in danger of losing control of the situation. He would have to act quickly or risk having an angry mob hand out their own rough justice. The ordinary man inside him, the man who liked a couple of pints with his mates, could quite happily step aside and let Harry mete out his own justice, but the police officer with eighteen years' experience knew he must act quickly. Before the situation got completely out of control. Sergeant Grove manhandled the now shaking and sweating Ashton into the rear seat of the patrol car and quickly closed the door.

Turning to the angry mob, the sergeant asked Harry, "Are you prepared to make a statement about what happened today, Sir?"

"You're bloody right I am."

Harry's reply was echoed by the other men.

"For his own safety, I'm taking this man into custody until I can be certain what actually happened here, I will arrange for another officer to come out here and take your statements."

As quickly as he could without risking another accident, he spun the car around and, with tyres throwing up plumes of dust, he turned out of the quarry and headed towards the police headquarters.

NINE

Allison was exhausted, mentally and physically. She had not had a proper night's sleep for days. Her mother's intuition told her that Jessica was ill. It didn't matter to her that the G.P. couldn't diagnose the problem. She knew, as only mothers can, that something was wrong. This was her fourth visit to the doctor, and she had made up her mind that she would not leave his surgery until he referred Jessica to the hospital.

Dr. Lomas was approaching retirement. He had been a GP for nearly forty years. In that time he had seen the National Health Service change out of all recognition. Now, budgets and targets seemed to take precedent over patient care. It was a situation that he wasn't happy with. Unlike some of his younger colleagues who had grown up with the present regime, he found himself unable to make the decisions that would invariably involve a large expenditure for the NHS. It went against his natural instincts to delay a child's treatment, but in his confused mind he had to stay within his budget.

The concern on Allison's face was obvious and her baby was clearly extremely ill. Too ill for him to delay any longer.

He telephoned the hospital and told them he was sending baby Jessica for further tests.

As she waited her turn at the hospital, Allison was relieved that now, at last, something would be done and poor Jessica would soon be a happy and smiling baby again.

In the warmth of the hospital, she allowed herself a few seconds to close her eyes and remember how happy and excited they had all been when they first moved into Hollybush Close.

After what seemed an eternity her name was called, and she carried Jessica into the examination room. Allison was taken by surprise at the doctor's appearance. He was a large, strong, rugged looking man. She imagined he could have been a rugby player, possibly even a biker. In fact, he reminded her of her own Graham and even without a word being spoken, she felt confident in his presence. It did not take him long to reach his diagnosis. Pneumonia. The mere sound of the word made Allison tremble. How could a tiny baby have pneumonia?

Allison was in a state of shock.

So many things to do. As the nurses made arrangements for Jessica to be admitted to the intensive care unit, she tried to calm herself. She was trying to put things into some sort of order.

"Yes, phone Graham first, then go to our baby. I have to stay with Jessica."

She tried to phone Graham but his mobile phone was dead. She couldn't hear it ringing and she couldn't leave a voicemail. Maybe he hadn't switched it on, maybe the battery was dead. Allison didn't have time for 'maybe'. Why do these things all conspire?

"Graham, sort your bloody phone out."

She had lost the ability to be calm. Right now, she wanted two things more than anything else in the world. She wanted baby Jessica to be well again and she wanted her husband there next to her, holding her hand. For the time being, she would have to cope on her own. As the nurses led her to the intensive care unit, they gave her a sterile cap and gown and reminded her that hospital regulations required that all mobile phones should be switched off. Allison shuddered as she realised just how alone she was at that moment.

TEN

O n the way to the quarry, the ambulance had travelled south down the motorway. The southbound traffic was relatively clear but the crew had noticed that the traffic travelling north on the other carriageway was slow and congested. They had also seen the number of large motor racing transporter lorries heading for Donington Park. As they had travelled south they hadn't known the full extent of the casualty's injuries but they had reasoned that any delay could have major implications. They also realised that it was very possible that they might be needed back at the circuit some time over the weekend.

Graham lay limp and seemingly lifeless in the ambulance. They had done what they could at the scene of the accident, but it was obvious that he was in a serious condition and he needed far more care than they were able to give. They had contacted the hospital by radio to give them an estimated time of arrival; they also gave a brief synopsis of his injuries. The ambulance crew knew that the first twenty minutes after an accident were absolutely crucial. If his condition could be stabilised within twenty minutes, he had a chance.

The ambulance station received the call at twelve minutes past three. They had arrived at the quarry at twenty-one minutes past three and left five minutes later. That left them just six minutes to get to the hospital fifteen miles away.

The journey took thirteen minutes and forty-two seconds.

The ambulance bay had been cleared and the driver reversed as close as possible to the Accident and Emergency suite, where the team of specialists were waiting. Graham's lifeless body was wheeled in and the race to save his life began.

It did not take them very long to realise that this might be a race they could not win.

All his life, Graham had been a fighter. At school he had fought the other kids. In adult life, he had fought for a decent life for himself and his family. At the quarry, every day was a fight just to earn a living and stay alive. Lying there unconscious with an army of doctors and nurses around him, he was in the middle of the biggest fight he had ever had.

Out in the corridor, the ambulance driver sat with his head in his hands. He tried to tell himself that this was just another day, just another job. He had done his best, now it was up to others. He had been in this position many times, too many, but this time the image that he saw over and over was not that of the casualty, it was the faces of the rescuers. Tough, hard men who earned their living working in a dangerous environment. The sort of men you might see in the pub having a few pints after work, laughing and joking with their mates and the sort of men you would probably want to avoid. He saw those faces streaked in tears and dust, their fingers ripped and bloodied and he saw the realisation in their eyes that this accident could have happened to any of them.

Whilst the crash team tried to establish the extent of Graham's injuries, his battered body was being monitored closely. His blood pressure and oxygen content were both falling. It was only too obvious that he had suffered massive internal injuries and suffocation under the weight of the gravel.

Eighteen minutes after being admitted, Graham suffered a massive heart attack and his fight was over.

"Thank you, team, you all did everything you could. Now we need to find out who he is and let his family know."

With that, the registrar began searching what was left of his clothing, trying to find any clues to his identity. He found his smashed mobile telephone, which was way beyond any use but he was able to extract the sim card. The heart of any cell phone that stores all the contact numbers that have been downloaded by the user. With the sim card fitted into his own phone, he was able to scan through the list of contact numbers, hoping that he might find a clue to a close relative. Luckily, there were not too many entries. He reasoned that numbers for doctors, garages and takeaways could all be discounted, as could those for names that sounded like friends. That left numbers for Allison and Mum. Allison's number was another cell phone, Mum's was a landline. He decided to try Mum first. With a heavy heart he waited while the phone rang but there was no reply and no voicemail. He had more luck with Allison's number; the receiver was switched off but he was able to leave a voicemail message asking her to call his extension at the hospital. He decided he would give Alison half an hour to reply before looking for other contacts.

One floor above, another life and death struggle was going on. Jessica's temperature had risen to a dangerous level and she was having trouble breathing. Allison had been ushered out of the small intensive care room to allow more nurses to attend to Jessica. Allison took the opportunity to switch on her phone and try once again to contact Graham.

ELEVEN

She didn't understand the message. Who was Dr. Khan and why was he trying to get in contact with her? She had walked out of the intensive care unit only seconds ago, surely there must be some mistake. She reassured herself that Dr Khan must be an administrator. Yes, that would be it. More forms to fill in. Holding the small cell phone with trembling fingers, she returned the call.

"Doctor Khan, Accident and Emergency department, speaking."

Alison was taken back by his reply and didn't know quite what to say. She composed herself enough to explain that she had called him as he had asked.

"I think it best if you can see me as soon as possible, and it might help if you can come with a friend. Do you know where the hospital is?"

"Yes, of course I know where it is. I've been here for hours with my little girl. Surely you know that she is in the intensive care unit. I'm standing outside it now."

"In that case," replied the doctor, "stay where you are and I'll be with you in a few minutes."

What is it with these hospital people? Don't they know anything? thought Alison.

Salman Khan was true to his word and in no time at all he was ushering her into a small side room. He was a slightly built man, probably in his early thirties, very smart, very correct, everything a doctor should be. Allison thought he looked the exact opposite of the rugby-playing biker doctor who was treating Jessica.

Slowly and tactfully, Dr. Khan explained that he had found her telephone number in the memory of a patient's cell phone and that he was anxious to identify the patient.

"I don't see how that affects me," replied Alison. "The only people who have my number are my husband and my mother and Mum lives miles away."

The words were fresh on her lips when she realised the implications of what she had said.

"Oh God! Don't let it be Graham. No. No."

Dr Khan tried to calm her down but she was totally distraught.

"Please can I see him? How badly is he hurt? Was it an accident at that bloody quarry? Please let me see him now. Please! Please!"

The doctor's words hit her like a bullet. A bullet that she was not expecting. And like a victim of a gunshot, she was totally destroyed. Her legs turned to jelly and she crashed to the floor in a heap. The nurses helped her to her feet and into a chair.

She was inconsolable. She was looking at the lifeless body of her husband. Her lover, her rock, her only ally in life's struggle. Gone. While, one floor above, just twenty feet away, her precious daughter was fighting for her life.

She returned to the intensive care unit and her baby.

She peered through the small windows. At first, she couldn't understand what she was looking at. There was no rush, no sense of urgency. The medical team appeared to be clearing away all the various life-saving equipment. One of the doctors saw her standing there and came over to her.

"I'm very sorry," he said, shaking his head.

Andrew Packford woke early; he had a lot to do, as he did every Saturday. He walked to the corner shop and bought a copy of the local newspaper. He always allowed himself time to read the paper as he ate breakfast. It was a small treat that he enjoyed before the work of restoring whatever he had managed to buy at the auction the day before. This week it would be the antique sewing table.

The front page carried the headline. "Young mother commits suicide."

Unfortunately, it's only deaths or celebrities that make the front cover of newspapers.

Andy read the article without the desperate circumstances really sinking in. It said that police had found Allison Jones' body in the home she had shared with her husband Graham and daughter Jessica. They had sealed off an area of Hollybush Close while they completed their investigations, but they were not looking for anyone else in connection with the death.

Their first thought was that she had committed suicide. A neighbour had raised the alarm just before midnight on Friday after hearing screams and sounds of sobbing coming from the property.

Andy flicked through the rest of the paper until an advertisement for the weekend's motor racing at Donington

Park caught his eye. He remembered seeing the trucks and transporters on the motorway the previous day. The prospect of seeing and hearing all those exotic cars being driven to the maximum by their millionaire owners pushed the sad headlines to the back of his mind.

Behind Andy's apartment was a row of lock-up garages. Most of them provided a home for unused bicycles or old washing machines; some, actually had cars in them, but not many. Most owners preferred to store a few pounds worth of junk in the garage while several thousands of pounds worth of motorcar stayed out in all weathers. Andy's garage doubled up as a workshop and storeroom. This morning it would be a workshop as he started to restore the old sewing table.

TWELVE

On race days, the paddock area at Donington Park is manic. Despite being enormous, it is never big enough. This is the area where the teams park the transporters and set up the awnings and corporate marquees. The days of drivers towing their racing car behind an old van ended sometime in the 1950s. Nowadays it's considered essential to have at least one lorry, a couple of quad bikes, at least one car and a motor home. The bigger the better. All painted in the colours of the team sponsor, unless, of course, you are wealthy enough not to need a sponsor.

Victor Manning didn't have a sponsor. Well, not a real one.

As with most things in his life, he was always sailing close to the wind. Always looking to push the boundaries of what is acceptable. Always looking for the extra pound, even if it meant cutting corners.

If you looked closely, you could see the small Viman logo on the side of the Mustang's door. To the casual observer it wouldn't mean much. But to Manning, it meant that he didn't have to go down on one knee to a sponsor. No appeasing some advertising director. No justifying the expenses. No sponsor praising speeches when he won. And he won with boring regularity. But that small logo was enough to satisfy the inland revenue that this was a justifiable expense. That he was spreading the public awareness of Viman Developments.

All his fun was tax deductible.

Howard Fryer had parked the lorry in a prominent position in the paddock. He knew that the spectators liked to look at the big Mustang and, more importantly, he knew that his boss liked to show it off, usually with the winner's trophy resting on the bonnet. In the unlikely event that there was no winner's trophy this weekend, the Mustang would be quickly hidden away inside the giant transporter.

Manning had arrived on Friday afternoon, completed a few laps of practice, set a respectable qualifying time and then driven the thirty or so miles back to Telcote Manor for a good night's sleep. He had left the mechanics to check the car over, adjust the fuel mixture, change the tyres, do all the things that make a car a winner. Then they could grab a hamburger from the stall and fall asleep in the back of the van.

He would eat his usual pre-race meal of veal escalope served on a bed of tagliatelle, washed down with a small glass of white wine. He retired early to bed and slept alone, leaving his wife in her bed while he thought of Angela and the Mustang, not necessarily in that order.

Manning woke early and drove back to Donington. He found Howard Fryer and his team relaxing with mugs of tea. They had finished checking the car and were taking the opportunity to chill out, unlike many of the other teams, which were still working feverishly on their cars. Manning liked to see the mechanics relaxing, to him, it meant that they had done their job properly. He knew how unsettling it was to climb into a car whilst it was still being worked on. He wouldn't admit it, but he knew that he owed most of his success to his team. His motor racing was not much different to his business success. He owed much of that to other people too.

Andy didn't rise quite so early; he didn't need to. When he was ready, he started work on the old sewing table that, with luck, would provide next week's wages. As he emptied the first drawer, he realised that someone had been using it until recently. Amongst the old buttons and long-forgotten silver thimbles were plastic cotton reels and shiny scissors. Andy tried not to think of the previous owner sewing buttons on her husband's shirt or adjusting a pair of trousers. Probably someone's wife, mother and granny, and now almost certainly dead.

When the drawer was empty, he lifted out the old newspapers that had been used to line it. As anyone would, he flicked through the pages and looking at the date, he realised the papers were nearly twenty years old. He assumed that was when the old table had been handed down to its previous owner or perhaps it had been cleaned out all those years ago. As he looked quickly at the old, yellowed pages, he stopped and stared at a photograph of two couples. Two men and their wives.

The caption beneath read, "Mr Victor Manning, Chairman of Viman Developments and Mr. Derek Harrison, Chief Planning Officer, together with their wives outside the latest housing project completed on time by Viman Developments".

One of the faces looked familiar to Andy and it took a few seconds for him to realise that Mrs. Derek Harrison, wife of the chief planning officer, was the same Mrs Harrison who had managed to outbid him at yesterday's auction.

He thought to himself, *she is an attractive woman now, twenty years ago, she was a stunner.*

With the first drawer emptied, he started on the second. It was very much the same. Old buttons, a couple of old pocketknives, scissors, and again, the bottom of the drawer lined with old newspapers. With slightly more enthusiasm, he read the old newspaper. Perhaps there were more photos of Mrs Harrison. If there were, he didn't see them. He did see a photograph of Victor Manning standing next to a row of new houses.

Andy thought, t*his fellow gets in everywhere.*

He briefly scanned the accompanying article without too much enthusiasm. The story seemed to imply that Viman Developments had built their latest development on land that the residents considered unsuitable for housing. The article covered the long-running dispute between on one side the developers, who, with the backing of the local planning department, were committed to going ahead with the building of a large housing estate, and on the other, the local residents, who were equally convinced that the land was waterlogged and contaminated by years of industrial use. Clearly the council and the developers had won the battle as the picture showed Manning standing proudly or should that be defiantly? outside the finished houses.

Andy didn't spend too much time reading the article. He had work to do and after all, what did he know about building land? But he could not help thinking that maybe the local residents knew more about the land than some suit in the planning department. He wondered what part Derek Harrison had played in the decision to build. He wondered briefly how the occupiers of the houses felt twenty years on. Dismissing all thoughts of houses and town planning and Mr Harrison, he carried on with his work on the sewing table. But the images of Mrs Harrison twenty years ago and yesterday at the auction stayed with him.

THIRTEEN

Sunday the eighteenth of March was bright and sunny. A bit cold but definitely bright. Andy joined the slow-moving queue waiting to enter Donington Park race circuit. Eventually he was inside the circuit and he parked his old BMW.

Andy's interest in motor racing had been born years ago when, as a thirteen year old, he and two mates had cycled to Mallory Park circuit, the "friendly circuit" as it's known locally. The spectacle of the cars racing around had left an impression on the young Andrew Packford, but more than the racing, the scene in the paddock area where the cars are prepared and looked after by the mechanics fascinated him. As a youngster he had seen his father tinker with the family car and in his own mind, he had been able to help by giving him the right sized spanner or by holding the end of a spinning bolt. But a race mechanic was in a different league. Waiting on the start line, surrounded by thirty other drivers, knowing that your mechanic has just replaced the brakes or adjusted the engine settings and being prepared to race flat out to the first corner, calls for a degree of confidence that most people can only hope for.

Since those early days, Andy's own mechanical ability had increased to the stage where he serviced and repaired his 750 Kawasaki motorbike, and with the same confidence he would be happy riding it to the maximum. Which he did regularly.

He reasoned that as it was still early in the day, he would tour the paddock area and watch the mechanics at work. The featured race of the weekend was for historic sports cars, the cars that most people can only dream of owning. Names like Aston Martin, Ferrari, Maserati, Alfa Romeo, Lotus, Chevrolet Corvette, Jaguar, Porsche and Ford Mustang. All well out of financial reach of most people.

As is the case of most motor racing events, there are always races for other classes of cars. Today, cheeky little Minis and humble Ford Escorts were sitting in the paddock alongside the main attractions, the historic sports cars. The paddock was beginning to fill up with enthusiasts moving from one car to another, looking, pointing and mostly taking photographs. Andy was no exception, following the crowd, going nowhere in particular. He was lost in thought, wondering in his own mind how any ordinary person could afford to go motor racing. Perhaps they were not ordinary. He wondered what ordinary was. His own thoughts were suddenly interrupted as the last person he expected to see walked across in front of him.

Mrs Derek Harrison, or Marie-Ann or whatever her name was, looked out of place in the race paddock that March morning. The tight-fitting jeans and knee-high leather boots offered no clue that the wearer was an antiques dealer or for that matter, the wife of the local town planning officer. Andy's first reaction was one of frustration.

He muttered to himself, "The auction is business but today is pleasure. Can't she leave me alone on my day off?"

But as she weaved her way between the race cars and the throng of enthusiasts, he realised that his eyes were still following her. More correctly, they were following the tight-itting jeans and the long boots. She may be an adversary in the saleroom, and she might be married to a suit at the town hall, and she might be a few years older than him, but in everyday language, he thought to himself that he could if she would.

Without thinking, he realised he was following her. It wasn't as if he was going anywhere in particular so it didn't really matter which way he went. Keeping a few yards back, he followed her until she pushed her way through the crowds and ducked under the barriers that were holding back rows of eager race enthusiasts hoping to get a look at the bright red Ford Mustang.

Unlike the other cars in the paddock area, the mechanics weren't working on the car, they were obviously satisfied that they had done all that they needed to do. As Andy peered through the crowd, he realised that he was looking at a very professional and experienced race team. Whilst the mechanics cleaned and sorted their tools at the back end of the huge transporter, Mrs Harrison joined two men sitting in the plush hospitality area at the front of the truck. Andy wondered what her connection was to the two men. One could have been her husband; he did bear some resemblance to the faded newspaper photograph he had looked at yesterday. Clearly the passing years had not been as kind to him as they had been to his wife. But who was the other guy?

A quick look at the race programme told him the car was entered by Viman Developments and the driver was Victor Manning. The name did not register at first. Why should it? He had forgotten the old newspaper and the photographs. He only remembered Mrs Harrison.

But as he looked at the expensive race team, he couldn't help but feel jealous. Jealous of the money and maybe jealous of this man's obvious connection with and closeness to Mrs Harrison.

Andy walked slowly away from the swarm of spectators around the Mustang. As he strolled around the busy race paddock, he wondered how the other competitors financed their cripplingly expensive hobby. Manning obviously built dubious housing estates, seemingly aided and abetted by Mr Harrison.

He found a good vantage point and settled down to watch the day's racing. But he found it difficult to get the Mustang and its driver and Mrs Harrison out of his mind.

Most of the races that day passed in a blur, that is, until Manning and the Mustang lined up on the front row of the starting grid. To his left there was a Maserati and to his right two Chevrolet Cameros, and behind, a whole host of expensive, noisy and frighteningly fast racing cars.

The red lights went out and the red mist came down as millions of pounds' worth of cars raced for the first bend. The ninety-degree Redgate Corner, where Andy watched as one of the Cameros led the pack through. Manning made a slow start and was in fifth position.

As they crossed the start line at the end of lap one, Manning had moved up to third and that's how he entered Redgate for the second time. The Camero was still in the lead, followed closely by the Birdcage Maserati. A funny name for a race car, but that was how they were known because the chassis was constructed with small-diameter tubes, hundreds of them, and of course, it resembled a birdcage.

They were lost to Andy's view until they came around again.

This time the three cars were side by side as they approached the bend, but only one would be on the right line to take the corner at speed. The Maserati driver was the first to brake, perhaps conscious of the enormous value of his car or perhaps it wasn't his car. Not an easy conversation to tell a wealthy owner that you have broken his pride and joy. Manning was now edging in front of the Camero and trying to force his car onto the correct line. He managed it, the Camero did not, siding off into the deep gravel, from where there was no escape.

Andy thought to himself, *that Manning is a tough bastard and is quite prepared to take what he wants.* Was he always like that or was it a skill he had developed? How do you develop into a tough bastard? Maybe he was born that way.

The racing continued and the laps went by. The Mustang stayed in front of the field of exotic, priceless race cars. When the chequered flag fell, signalling the end of the race, Manning and the Mustang were the clear winners.

Andy felt that Manning had bulldozed his way to victory, pushing any opponents out of his way. There was no finesse, no camaraderie, no being one of the boys. Just the need to win. He didn't like that. Maybe he could see some of himself in Manning.

Maybe, if he was really pushed, he could be as ruthless. The thought scared him.

FOURTEEN

The next few days passed like any others. Andy put the motor racing and Victor Manning to the back of his mind. But the vision of Mrs Harrison stayed with him as he continued with the restoration of his stock of antiques. When Friday came around again, he made his way to Miller and Jackman auction rooms, as he did every week. As usual, he settled down with a cup of coffee while he waited for the auctioneer to offer something that he might be interested in.

Whilst he waited, he casually looked through a well-read newspaper that someone had discarded. It had been left folded over and as he opened the creased pages, his attention was focussed on the main story."Family of three die on the same day in separate incidents".

Andy realised the connection between this story and the earlier one regarding the apparent suicide. As he read, he realised how their sad lives were so different from his own and how massively they contrasted with the lives of the people he had been watching a few days before at the racing circuit.

He couldn't get the images out of his mind. The image

of a hard working, normal, whatever that is young man, working in the harshest of environments and coming to that end. Buried under tons of wet slimy gravel, and for what? Was it to fulfil the need to build new houses or was it to make money for all those people involved in building new homes? Was it for making money so that someone could go motor racing? Something stirred inside Andy. He didn't know it then, but the feeling of unease was building up inside him and it would remain with him for a long time.

His mind was not really on antiques. He was trying to imagine what it would be like going to work every day knowing that you might end up under the very same gravel that you had dug up and moved day after day. How could his wife cope with knowing what her partner had to endure so that they could maintain their very basic way of life?

He left the saleroom early. He hadn't bought anything. He didn't really try. He was finding it difficult to focus on anything other than Graham Jones lying under that moving, creeping, sliding, all enveloping mass, and his wife trying to cope with a terminally sick child. And the reality that finally she couldn't cope. As Andy walked to his car, he caught sight of Mrs Harrison loading something into her van. He decided not to talk to her, not to mention that he had seen her in very different circumstances a couple of days ago. Before he could walk past, she turned and saw him. He found himself returning the smile and nod of the head, the small gestures that say, 'I don't want to ignore you but I'm not ready to be friends'

Andy drove slowly out of the car park and turned onto the main road. It wasn't a conscious decision to load Hollybush Close into the SatNav, he just found himself doing it. Anyway, as it happened, it wasn't far off his route. He felt the need to know more about the dead family. Looking at the family home might help.

The entry roads to the estate were very impressive. Large four- and five-bedroom houses, nice gardens, large cars. Just the sort of people that might collect antiques, possibly some of Andy's customers lived here. But Hollybush Close was a bit different.

He wondered which was their house, but that question was soon answered. As he steered round a bend in the road, the small house facing him was hidden behind a wall of flowers. As he looked on, small children holding their mother's hand were laying their own tributes. Single flowers, large bunches, wreaths and wildflowers picked from the fields lay side by side. Teddy bears, dolls, children's rattles. Everyone laid by someone who cared.

He parked the car and walked over. As he read the messages attached to the tributes, many were misspelled or badly written, but they were all genuine messages of sympathy placed there by genuine people. Just like the unfortunate dead family. A young mother cradling her baby in her arms asked Andy if he was a friend of the family or another bloody journalist. He said he was neither, just somebody who was moved by the sad story.

"Well, somebody needs to pay for this. This was an accident waiting to happen, she snapped back."

Andy didn't really understand her anger. Of course, the deaths of three people, a complete family, were sad beyond words. He wasn't sure how to ask the question that was in his thoughts. He could understand a distraught mother killing herself after the death of her husband and their only child, but what lay behind it all? Was it just a coincidence or was there some connection?

"I've read the story in the newspaper; I only know what has been written. Is there something more?" he asked."I'm not sure if I'm in a position to help, but it may help you to get it off your chest."

Less than twenty miles away, Derek Harrison was addressing the local council planning committee.

"In order that we meet our housing targets, it is essential that this proposal by Viman Developments gets the go ahead, I know that some members of the committee have their reservations about the suitability of the site, but I have assurances from Viman that they have carefully surveyed the area and they are confident that the small amount of contamination can be successfully contained, and with the right treatment, completely eradicated."

The committee discussed the proposal amongst themselves. They knew the council was under pressure from the government to increase their housing stock, and they also knew that Viman had successfully turned similar contaminated sites into showcase developments. There was no reason why this site would be any different.

As usual in these cases, all the surveys, all the treatments, were notional. They were all desk surveys, as they are called. That means all the checks were done on a computer, if the computer failed to reveal anything too bad then the site must be alright. Of course, the computer didn't know that local residents had been suffering with breathing problems for years. Problems caused by the filth belching out of the foundry chimneys that had previously stood on the site. No one thought to ask the local residents. Well, maybe they did and maybe they didn't want to hear the answers.

The committee listened to their planning officer. Why shouldn't they? He was the expert. A highly paid expert.

Whilst most members of the planning committee were in agreement with the proposals, there were those who had their doubts, so the chairman informed the committee that a final decision would be postponed until Viman had submitted further details at the next scheduled meeting.

Andy listened to the young mother as she told him about her neighbours, Graham and Alison and their baby daughter Jessica, their lives and their subsequent deaths. He was a good listener. Usually it was a customer wittering on about their collection of thimbles or whatever. But this was different because he wanted to hear her.

He wanted to help.

The anger and frustration were clearly building up inside her. Andy sensed the desperation in her voice.

"I realise you have your hands full looking after your baby, but is there a chance we could talk a little more?" Andy asked.

"I suppose you could come back to mine and I'll make us a cup of tea."

As he sat in the small living area surrounded by all the stuff babies need, pushchairs, bouncers, toys he realised that this young mother lived a totally different life to his. A small part of him was jealous but he realised that she was a prisoner of her own making. Her life was so different to the freedom he enjoyed and needed.

He heard the kettle boiling and stepped into the kitchen to see if he could help. It was small, like the living room. The sink was clean but the Formica work surfaces were dirty and chipped, the cupboards were badly fitted and a couple of doors were hanging precariously on their hinges.

The most striking feature was the smell. Not the smell of a baby, but the smell of decay. His eyes scanned the room. It didn't take more than a few seconds before they found the cause.

There was a large black mass of mould. A filthy, furry mass of smelly mould. It spread along the wall above the sparse cupboards and across the ceiling. For once he was lost for words. Should he mention it? Maybe she never cleaned the place. He kept quiet and helped carry the teacups into the lounge.

"I saw you looking, "she said. "At the mould. That first appeared a few weeks after we moved in. We've cleaned it off, but it just comes back, almost as quickly as we clean it. And the smell! You should try living with it twenty-four seven."

For once Andy didn't know what to say.

"Are all the houses like this?"

"They are at this end of the estate. I doubt if those posh houses are like it but I don't know anyone who has been inside one of those. This is what killed my neighbours."

By now her voice was beginning to break. She went on to explain that baby Jessica had developed a cough that kept the family awake at nights and that, despite frequent visits to the doctors, they had been unable to cure it.

"I don't know what happened that day, but I do know that Graham and Alison didn't get any sleep for weeks. He had been late for work so many times that he was scared he would get the sack. I think he either fell asleep at work or tried to cut corners. Either way, it doesn't matter, he's dead now. They're all bloody dead."

Andy didn't want to push it, he knew she was close to breaking point but there were still some questions that needed answers.

"I don't want to jump to conclusions, but I assume this house is rented, have you contacted the landlord?"

"Of course, we have, it's owned by a housing association and frankly, they couldn't give a toss, so long as they get their rent, that's all they care about and if we don't like it there are plenty more waiting to move in."

Andy needed a moment to collect his thoughts. He guessed the houses weren't very old, probably not more than two or three years.

"Have you tried to contact the builder? He must take some responsibility."

"Now you are joking! The bastard couldn't care less. You see his photo in the newspapers every week, showing off his latest building site, but he won't go near his old ones. I hate him and what he has done to us. I'd dance on his grave."

"Who was the builder?" Andy asked.

"A bunch of money grabbing cowboys called Viman, led by the biggest crook of all Victor Manning!"

Andy knew the conversation was over.

FIFTEEN

Some employers like to think of themselves as being one of the lads, shirt sleeves rolled up, walking around with a cup of tea in their hand.

Others consider themselves above that sort of thing and take the autocratic approach. Amongst the autocratic bosses, there are two schools of thought, those who position their desk on a plinth so that the employee must look up to them, god-like, and those who sit comfortably behind a large, tidy, well-polished desk whilst lesser mortals stand nervously in front of them. This second approach has two advantages. Firstly, there is no doubt who is in charge, none at all. And secondly, when authority needs to be displayed, it is so easy to stand and literally thump the table.

Victor manning was sitting comfortably. The others were standing.

"For Christ's sake, let's get our act together. The planning committee is meeting again next week, and we need to get this through without any more delays."

Manning was not in the mood for polite conversation.

"What is so special about this site that we can't sort it?"

The question was not directed at anyone in particular, but each of his five planning advisors took it personally. Finally, one of them spoke.

"This site is a bit different to the others. It has been used as a foundry for the past sixty years. We have the double problems of site contamination from the actual processes and from the waste products. Despite Mr Harrison's support, some members of the planning council had their doubts. That's why it was deferred. To be certain of getting it approved, we would need a clean bill of health. To get that, we would need to excavate to a much greater depth, probably several metres, and then there is the cost of disposing of the contaminated soil. Under EU reg."

"Do I look like I care about the EU? I'm not building houses in bloody Brussels! Why can't we just scrape the topsoil and add a few more green spaces to satisfy the tree huggers? It's worked before. You write it up, make it sound good. I'll make sure Harrison gets it passed."

The five men walked slowly out of his office. They knew from experience that there were times to make a point and there were times to walk away.

Manning buzzed the intercom and Angela came in.

"Regulations for this and bloody regulations for that. If we all followed the regulations, nothing would get done. I need a drink."

"You sound like you need more than a drink," she said.

The drinks cabinet was in the corner of the office, underneath the photograph of him and the Mustang with the winner's garland at Silverstone. She poured a generous measure of Scotch into a cut-glass tumbler and a smaller one for herself.

Manning had moved from behind his desk and was sitting on the leather Chesterfield directly opposite the drinks cabinet. As she crossed the room the sound of her high heels was lost in the thickness of the carpet. She leaned over him to place his drink on the side table. As she did, she knew he would look down her blouse like a naughty schoolboy might take a quick glance at his teacher's bosom. She sat next to him, not quite touching but tantalisingly close. He said nothing. She ran her hand over his shoulder and down his arm. He said nothing. She let her fingers rest on the belt of his trousers. He still said nothing. She unzipped his trousers.

It was quickly over.

He stood up and rearranged his clothing. She finished her drink.

"I've got work to do. Get Harrison to come and see me he needs to start earning his money."

Angela returned the empty glasses and silently walked out of the office.

Back in his apartment, Andy could not settle. He had plenty of things he could get on with. Plenty of stock to restore or clean, plenty of stock to sell. It was not as if he didn't need the money. But when he compared his safe, organised life to the lives of those families living on Hollybush Close, he wondered how many other similar estates there were, how many other families lived in conditions that would eventually threaten their health.

How could Victor Manning spend thousands of pounds on his motor-racing hobby while his houses were causing such distress to others? How could any man do that?

For once Andy was out of his depth. He knew nothing

about building houses, nothing about damp and mould, nothing about planning procedures. The feeling of uselessness hung over him. It weighed him down like a giant rock on his shoulders. Then, slowly at first, he compared his current position with the one he was in three years ago. He left a well-paid job with a regular salary to become an antiques dealer, a career that he knew very little about.

What did he know then about auctions, about profit margins? Nothing! He listened to other people, checked things out for himself and came to his own conclusions. Sure, he had made mistakes, but he had learned from them. Maybe he could use the same approach again.

The more he thought about it, the more it made sense.

He knew he was developing a dislike of Victor Manning. He had seen both sides of him and didn't particularly like either. If he had to choose between the winner's champagne in Manning's hospitality transporter at Donington Park or a cup of tea at Hollybush Close, the Close would win every time.

Andy started at the local council's planning department's website. He concentrated on the applications made by Viman Developments in the past three years. It was not a long list, but presumably long enough to provide Manning with the lifestyle to which he was accustomed. He quickly found the original application for what was now the estate that included Hollybush Close. The plans included four and five bedroom detached houses, three bedroomed semi-detached and two rows of terraced houses. Hollybush Close.

Attached to the application, there were various surveys from the utility companies, the local transport co-ordinators, schools etc all very boring and all in favour of the 'very much needed' new houses. Andy didn't know how these things worked, but he reasoned that no developer would include any surveys that might oppose his plans.

It took a long time to find it. In fact, if he were more familiar with the process he might well have flicked through the papers and skipped over it. But hidden in the small print was the fact that the site had originally been owned by Jaden Plating Ltd.

He Googled Jaden Plating on his computer. It emerged that the company had closed down two years before Viman's application. For those two years, the old buildings had stood empty and derelict. The local kids had played there and there was plenty of evidence that local residents had repeatedly complained to the council to clean up the area. The further he delved into Jaden, the murkier the picture was. The company closed after more than twenty years in business as industrial platers. The closure was due in part to pressure from local residents about the fumes and the failure of the company to take any notice of the repeated demands of the health and safety inspector.

Andy knew very little about planning, but he knew a fair bit about buying and selling. Whether antiques or land, the principle is the same. The seller has to sell for the most they can whilst the buyer has to buy for the least they can.

It is easy. A business that has effectively been closed down by the health and safety inspector is not worth much. And land that has been contaminated over a long period is worth very little. But the same land with a nice new housing estate and a few green spaces might be worth millions.

The triple deaths were the only newsworthy events so the local paper was still covering the story. The latest article ended by informing readers that a preliminary inquest would be held into the deaths.

Andy was struggling now. Did anyone else know about the old plating works? Would the contamination have had any effect on the residents? Should he tell anyone? *Who* should he tell? Did the authorities already know? Too many questions. He decided, as he always did, to take one step at a time.

The phone rang in the coroner's office. After the usual introductions, Andy explained his position. He was an involved member of the public. He had information that he thought might be of interest to the coroner's hearing and the possible verdict. Was he an expert? Well no, he wasn't, but he was prepared to state what he had found out and an expert could make a decision about it. He reasoned that it was the least he could do for three dead people he had never met. Three dead people who were beginning to take over his life.

Andy drove back to Hollybush Close. He parked his car at the far end of the Close. He stood back and looked around, not knowing what he was looking for. He rather hoped that something would look out of place, maybe unusual, something that might give him a clue to the previous occupier of the site. But there was nothing.

There were terraced houses, with small, barren front gardens, mainly littered with discarded children's toys, and not much else. Surely if this land were contaminated there would be some signs, but there was nothing. As he stood and looked, a front door opened. It was not the house he had been invited into for tea but a neighbour. As one child opened the front door, a sibling opened the back door into the garden, giving Andy a clear view front to back. That's when he realised that he had missed the signs. They had been staring him in the face, but he had missed them. The obvious sign was that there was nothing in the gardens, front or rear.

They were completely devoid of any vegetation.

The child at the front door was quickly followed by his mother, ever eager to protect her children. She viewed Andy with a certain amount of suspicion. He introduced himself as someone who was concerned about the recent deaths of her neighbours. She did not seem convinced. Why would a complete stranger be interested in the tragedy? The conversation was one-sided. As Andy told her what he knew of the previous use of the site and of his intention to prove to the coroner that the site was not suitable for human habitation, she began to trust him. He was probably the first person to try to help them.

"Do you manage to grow anything in your garden?" Andy asked.

"Not a thing. Everything dies, even the kid's attempts to grow Sunflowers you know, like they do at school. Everything dies eventually. I don't know who you are, mister, but if you think you can take on the builders and the council, I wish you luck! I wasn't at all sure about you, but you sound like a good bloke. Just mind how you go."

Mind how you go! It had been a long time since anyone had said that to Andy. People say it all the time but he didn't really know what it meant, and he didn't know it would come back to haunt him.

He returned to his car and drove out of the estate. He turned left and left again, bringing him behind the new houses. The houses here were much older, probably built just after the First World War. Some had been well maintained and were a credit to their owners; others looked very neglected. Andy reasoned that these houses might be occupied by elderly residents. Residents that might have lived in the area for a long time. Residents that might remember Jaden Plating.

An elderly lady was putting rubbish in her dustbin. As she looked up, she saw Andy standing by her garden gate.

"I don't buy nothing at the door and I can't afford double glazing," She said as she turned and started to walk back into her house.

Not wanting to alarm her, Andy stayed where he was and called after her. "Please can you spare me a minute? I just want to talk about the old plating works."

"Why would anyone want to talk about that place? It's been gone for years and good riddance, that's what I say. That place was a death trap."

"That's why I want to talk about it." Andy replied.

"Well, I suppose you better come in, don't be standing on the doorstep like that. You're sure you're not trying to sell me anything?"

"No, honestly, I just want to talk."

She ushered him inside and offered him a well-worn chair. Andy explained that he had heard about the deaths of the Jones family and thought that there might be a connection between the tragedy and the new housing estate that had been built on the old plating works.

SIXTEEN

Andy was nervous. This was a new sensation for him. Once again, he found himself out of his depth and he knew it. What should he say? How should he say it? Well, he would just take it one step at a time, like he did everything. After all, the people he would be talking to were just like him, they got dressed every day and pulled their trousers on one leg at a time, just like him.

The coroner opened the proceedings by outlining the events on that March day. His opening statement asked the question if the three deaths were somehow connected or if they were just a cruel coincidence. He concluded by saying that he hoped the court would come to the correct decision.

First, the court would hear about the death of Graham Jones.

Sergeant John Grove told the coroner what he had seen at the quarry. His testimony was backed up by a statement from the health and safety inspector condemning the working conditions on the site. Before coming to any conclusions, the coroner moved on to the death of baby Jessica. After the medical evidence was heard, the coroner's clerk called Andrew Packford.

"Are you here in an official capacity, Mr Packford? Do you have qualifications relevant to the events?" The coroner asked.

"No sir, I have no qualifications, but I have spoken in depth to people who are in some way connected to these events, and I have found various disturbing facts concerning the lives of these three people that may have contributed to their deaths, and I think the court should be aware of them."

"Very well, you may make a statement, but please keep it brief."

Andy started by describing the conversation he had had with the Jones' neighbour, how the houses suffered from fungus and mould growth and how that in turn had damaged Jessica's health. He continued, "I have researched the previous history of this site and found that it was empty for two years before the developers bought it, before that, it had been used by an industrial plating company for twenty years. Without undertaking a comprehensive survey, it's very difficult to say what pollutants there may be in the soil, but it's very likely to include chromium, nickel and cadmium deposits, which can cause lung cancer and kidney damage also pulmonary oedema. I had a long discussion with Mrs Wilkins. She is an eighty one year old lady who has lived in a house bordering the old factory for many years. She was well aware of the health risks as her husband worked for Jaden Plating and subsequently contracted lung cancer and died. I would respectfully suggest to this court that the pollutants contributed to the ill health of Jessica, which in turn resulted in her father operating dangerous machinery whilst he was suffering extreme tiredness. In the light of the previous industry and the contamination, my opinion is that house building should never have been permitted on that site."

Andy sat down to cheers from the public gallery. Voices echoed around the room. "Good on yer mate! Thank you. Thank you!"

Andy looked around to see some of the residents of Hollybush Close. After their initial doubts, it made him feel very humble that at last, they felt they could trust him. Maybe they had been shafted by society for so many years that they had forgotten how to trust.

"Silence! in this courtroom!" shouted the coroner. "Thank you, Mr Packford. At this stage I don't know if your assumptions are correct or not, but I am going to adjourn this inquest until I can get statements from all the other parties and from independent specialists."

With that, the courtroom emptied. As Andy left, he was chased by the reporter from the local newspaper.

"If I buy you a beer can we talk for a bit?"

The day was beginning to weigh heavy on Andy. A few hours ago he was just an anonymous bloke in the street. Now he had opened a can of worms in a coroner's court and been cheered on by the gallery. Now he was being pursued by the press. He didn't know it, but this was only the beginning.

The pub wasn't very busy, Andy and the reporter had no trouble finding a quiet table.

"You do know who built the houses, don't you?" the reporter asked, not waiting for a reply. He answered his own question. "Viman Developments. That's Victor Manning's firm."

"Does it matter who built them? They either knew what they were doing and didn't care, or they didn't know. Either way, they shouldn't be in the business of building homes for people who are not in a position to be choosey about where they live. People who trust builders and housing associations to provide safe, comfortable houses for their families."

Andy listened to himself and realised he was in danger of becoming a crusader. Perhaps he had already crossed that line.

"Victor Manning is a man used to getting his own way. I wish you luck, but you just mind how you go."

"Just mind how you go!" This was the second time Andy had heard that particular expression. The first time it came from a concerned neighbour and he took it as a friendly token; the second time it sounded like a warning.

Manning paced back and forth across his office, not going in any particular direction, which didn't make it easy for the others who were trying to get out of his way. He held the folded and crumpled newspaper like a weapon, slapping whoever happened to be in front of him.

"Where did this bloody journalist get his story from and who is this bloke who stirred up the coroner with this pack of lies?"

Viman's team of designers and planners stood there like schoolchildren. No one spoke. Everyone in that office knew how things worked. They designed the houses, they planned the estate layouts and squeezed in as many houses as possible. But Victor Manning paid their wages. It was Victor Manning who made the important decisions and it was he who was ultimately responsible for what was built and, more importantly, where it was built. Victor Manning was the general and they were his foot soldiers. No more, no less.

Historically, generals have a knack of passing the buck down the ranks.

Even if they knew, no one answered his question. The silence that hung over the room was broken by the sound of breaking glass, followed by shrieks and screams coming from his secretary's office.

Manning was visibly shaken. "What the bloody hell was that?" he screamed. As he rushed towards the front of the small office building, his secretary and the other ladies working at Viman Developments were retreating to the rear of the building.

Manning was alone at the front door of the building and facing an angry mob led by Harry Thornton.

"You bastard." He spat at Manning. "If it's not enough that you build shit houses, you build them with sand and gravel from that bloody quarry, I know, I've delivered to enough of your sites to know what goes on. You killed my mate Graham and his family. I hope they have finally caught up with you."

Manning slammed the door on the angry mob and returned to the relative sanctuary of his office. His staff were still there, standing in stunned silence. For once their boss was lost for words.

SEVENTEEN

Friday. Auction day at Miller and Jackman. Andy parked his car as usual and made his way to the saleroom via the coffee stall. He squeezed between the crowds of potential buyers looking at the various lots offered for sale. As he made his way around the display tables, he was lost in the desire to try to make a living. Carefully thinking about what such an item might sell for and what he could pay for it to leave himself with a modest margin of profit. He was shaken out of his thoughts by a gentle tap on his shoulder.

"It was you I saw at Donington the other week, wasn't it? We were there with my husband's friend Vic, he was racing his Mustang. We usually go with him if he's racing locally."

"Yes, Mrs Harrison, it was me, I was surprised to see you there. I wouldn't have thought motor racing was your thing."

"Please call me Susan. After all, we do see each other here on sale days. Oh yes, I love the thrill of car racing. The idea of man-to-man conflict, it's a bit gladiatorial, don't you think?"

"Yes, I suppose so, but I'm more interested in the technical side of things. Anyone can be a gladiator with a few million pounds in the bank."

"Spoken like an unromantic man. Where's your sense of gentlemanly competition?"

"I didn't see your friend Victor Manning show much gentlemanly competition, only brute force and a desire to be a winner at any costs."

"Isn't that a bit like you, MrPackford? You like to be a winner in the saleroom."

"No, you've got me wrong, I'm not interested in winning, my only interest is trying to make a decent living. Unlike a lot of others here today, buying and selling antiques is my only way to pay the bills. If I don't buy the right items at the right price, I don't make any money. If I don't make money, I don't eat. Simple as!"

"Please don't be like that! It sounds like you are having a go at me. I do take things very seriously, you know. It would be nice if we could both be friends. After all, we do have a lot in common, well, antiques and motor racing for starters, and who knows what else?"

'Who knows what else?' was said with a sparkle in her eye and the significance of that wasn't lost on Andy. She might be a few years older than him and she might keep company with dubious builders, but she was a very attractive lady.

"Why don't we have a coffee together after the sale and we can find out if we have any other mutual interests?"

"Okay, why not?" Andy relented. "I'll catch you later. Now I have things to buy and a living to Make."

With that they went their separate ways.

Two hours later and the auction finished, Andy found her waiting for him as he collected the various bits he had managed to buy.

"Are you ready for that coffee now? I certainly am. I know a nice quiet café a short drive from here. You can tell me all about yourself."

Andy followed the little van and parked behind it, outside a very chic, modern café. He imagined it was the sort of café where the local ladies would meet for coffee. It certainly was not the type of establishment where the local builders would get their morning tea.

They settled into a leather Chesterfield, towards the back and out of sight of any passer-by who might look in out of curiosity.

"My name is Susan. What should I call you? I can't keep calling you 'Mr Packford."

"Andy. Everybody calls me Andy."

"Well, Andy, you seem very confident in the saleroom. How long have you been in the antiques business?"

"About three years now. It was hard at first but I gradually found my feet and now I love it. I can't imagine doing anything else. I might seem confident in the saleroom and when I am dealing with customers, but in the beginning I was a nervous wreck. I found that all the established dealers wanted to keep it as a closed shop. Pretending that you had to be in the business for years before you earned the right to be a dealer. All that is bullshit. Anyway, I thrive on a challenge. If I'm ever told something can't be done, I have to prove them wrong. And we all know that a journey of a thousand miles starts with the first step."

"You know, Andy, I completely misjudged you. I had you down as a Jack the Lad character, you know, a bit of a chancer. But you're not, are you? You're sincere and deep thinking. I like that."

"That's funny because I had you down as a chancer, running an antiques shop with your husband's money backing you, just to prove to him that you could do it. And, of course, to keep you busy while he is at work all day."

"You cheeky young upstart!" she said with a smile on her lips. "I've been doing this for years. Well, at least ten. And you are right, it is the best way to earn a living. I have been trying to get my husband to take early retirement and join me in the shop. We would make a good team, I know that. But I don't think it will happen, he's too absorbed in his own career. He is the chief planning officer for the local council and I think he might be too old to change now. Boardrooms to auction rooms is a big step."

Andy wasn't sure if he should tell her about the old newspapers he had found, or the fact that he knew who her husband was and what he did for a living. He also realised that if he continued to help the residents of Hollybush Close, he might find himself in direct conflict with Victor Manning and, quite possibly, Mr Derek Harrison. He was enjoying relaxing and talking to Susan. He never found it easy to make friends with other antique dealers as he considered them as competitors. Why would you be friendly with someone in the same line of business as yourself? But she was different and, despite his early reservations and the fact that he had thought she was only playing at the business with her husband's money, he realised that they had a lot in common. And he realised he liked her.

Their conversation continued over a second cup of coffee. The more they talked, the more they began to enjoy each other's company. To a casual observer, they might have been a couple who had met on the internet and were having their first real date. Maybe that's what they *were* having.

They talked like excited teenagers, asking each other ever more prying questions. Some personal, some business related. Susan was thoughtful for a few seconds then, out of the blue, she offered Andy a proposition.

"I've really enjoyed our talk and I feel we have a lot in common. Why don't we work together? Well, perhaps not actually together, as I get the impression that we are both free spirits and we each value our independence, but we could help each other."

"What do you have in mind?" asked Andy.

"Well, for starters, I don't have the ability to restore old furniture. I know you can, You could do my restorations and in exchange I could sell some of your stock in my shop. That way you will always have something to work on and earn money, while I will have some new and different stock."

He didn't have to think too hard. Although he generally kept busy, he did have some spare time and the prospect of filling that time profitably while someone else sold his stock was quite appealing.

"Okay. That sounds like a plan. Let's do it."

They exchanged telephone numbers and agreed to make contact again in the next few days to finalise things. Leaving the café, Susan linked her arm in his and looking like a married couple he walked her to her little van. He sat in his BMW and watched her drive away. The time spent in the café, just sitting and talking, reminded Andy of happy times he had spent with his wife, but the enjoyment of the afternoon was tinged with the sad memory of his broken marriage.

EIGHTEEN

The doors to the council chambers opened at seven p.m. sharp.

The public were always welcome to attend meetings of the planning committee, but they rarely bothered. There was very little excitement in listening to the latest planning applications, which usually involved some house owner wanting to build an extension or a new garage. Occasionally local interest might be aroused or offended if a proposed development overstepped the mark and had a detrimental effect on another property, but generally the only people there were those directly involved, usually the applicant and his team of advisors.

Viman Developments had sent their senior planning officer, Mark Seymour, to present their latest plans for their new housing development. He had been in this position many times before. He would give the planning committee the outline details of his proposal, backed up with reports from the local utility companies that would confirm that there were no reasons whatsoever why the new houses should not be built. They could, of course, handle another one hundred and fifty new customers.

Of course, they could.

And of course, these badly needed new homes would help the local council meet their housing requirements. He did not actually say that if this development was passed. Victor Manning would stand to make another seven million pounds to add to his already considerable fortune. Or that the future of his own career might depend on a favourable outcome. His plans had the backing of the council's own chief planning officer so he had no reason to expect that it would be anything but an easy hearing.

Seymour took his seat and shuffled his papers into the correct order, ready to answer any questions the committee might fire at him.He was surprised to see a steady stream of local residents walk nervously in and take their seats.

The chairman opened the proceedings by explaining that a decision on this particular proposal had been deferred from the previous meeting and that now the applicant would present more detailed plans and further information regarding the suitability of the site. He went on to explain to the bemused audience that the final decision would be made by the twelve councillors who sat on the planning committee after they had heard all the evidence for and against the plans.

Seymour took to his feet and outlined Viman Developments' plans to build an estate of one hundred and fifty new homes on an old, long-abandoned brownfield site. That is to say, a site that previously had some kind of building or buildings on it. He was careful to emphasise that by building on a brownfield site, the development would not endanger green belt land, which is obviously so important to protect.

He made a compelling argument. The council needed more new houses, his company could provide them without damaging green spaces and at the same time put an old, disused eyesore of a site to good use. He went on to state that the scheme had the full backing of the council's own chief planning officer, Mr Derek Harrison. He went on to show the committee copies of letters from utilities companies who also backed the plans. The local schools had plenty of scope for more pupils, there were local bus routes, a doctor's surgery not far away. At this point he thought he was home and dry.

Out of the corner of his eye he could see councillors nodding agreement. It was in the bag.

When Seymour finally sat down, the chairman asked the members of the public if anyone wanted to address the meeting. There was an unexpected flurry of hands waving at him, all wanting their chance to raise their objections. The first to speak introduced himself as Harry Thornton.

"I've never been to a meeting like this before and I don't know how I should address you. To be honest, I am a normal working man. I drive a tipper lorry for a living and I never had the education that most of you folks here have had, but I certainly have a few things I would like to get off my chest."

"Please carry on, Mr Thornton. I doesn't really matter how you address any of us, so long as your observations are valid."

"Oh, they're valid, alright! Mr Seymour here, will have us all believing that Victor Manning is a saint. What with building all these lovely new houses an' all. But have any of you folks looked at his houses when they are a few years old? Have you read the newspapers about the deaths of the Jones family, who were living in one of the houses that he'd built? I worked with Graham Jones and he told me about the state of his house and how it had affected his little girl. How she was struggling to breathe and crying all the time, all of it caused by the damp and fungus that grew in that house. All caused by him building on the site of an old plating works. Anyone with any sense knows that the fumes and contamination left behind are deadly. Now Victor manning is trying to build on the site of an old foundry. God alone knows what sort of rubbish has been left there."

"Thank you, Mr Thornton. I think we are all aware of the sad events you talked about but I don't think they apply to this particular application. I am sure you appreciate that we cannot discuss any previously agreed applications; we can only listen to comments that are specific to this new development. Does anyone else have anything to say?"

Harry didn't know how to respond. He knew he had made his point but he had clearly been talked down. In his own world he would have coped but now he was in a world he didn't really understand, so with reluctance he sat down.

Next to get the chance to speak was Andy. He had seen the meeting mentioned in the local newspaper a few days earlier and he had made the obvious connection between this new proposal and his visits and talks to the residents of Hollybush Close. Although he didn't consider himself an expert, he was fast realising that by not sharing what he knew about Viman, he was in effect condoning their actions.

"My name is Andrew Packford and I feel compelled to follow up on the comments made by the previous speaker. Whilst I appreciate that they are two totally different building sites, they are joined by the same thread. This developer has a history of building on contaminated sites. In my opinion, building on this particular site should be prohibited until it has been checked by independent experts."

When he first started to speak, Packford felt like an outsider, somebody who should not be there. However, the more he spoke, the more he felt that he had the attention of the planning committee, the decision makers. He was careful to look around and try to establish eye contact with them, trying to make some kind of connection. In reality, he didn't have to worry; he was a big man with a large presence and he already had their attention.

He continued. "I have done some very basic research on the internet, something that the council's planning department should have done in more depth. This proposed development is on the site of an old foundry. Firstly, since 1999, councils have had a responsibility to register all sites that may be contaminated. Secondly, foundries contaminate land in several ways. There's surface contamination from waste sand and contamination from polycyclic aromatic hydrocarbons that can be absorbed into the soil and the watercourse. I am far from being an expert, but in short, the whole proposal is a farce. It should be rejected out of hand, and quite frankly, the council needs to look at its own planning procedures and protocol to make sure that this kind of thing never happens again."

The chairman of the meeting did not know whether Andy had finished his speech or not. The council chambers were in uproar. Members of the public were on their feet; some of them were congratulating Andy, some were cheering, some were clapping.

Mark Seymour was not doing any of those things. He was frantically flicking through his papers, trying to find some basis for a reply. At that moment he would have chosen to be anywhere except where he was. If the plans were rejected, he would have to explain to Victor Manning what went wrong. He tried to save the situation. Very gingerly he rose to his feet.

"Please. PLEASE! Can I address this meeting? Of course, the points this gentleman has raised are known to us and we have taken appropriate steps in our design and build strategy to mitigate the problem. I represent a responsible and reputable developer who would never knowingly do anything that might result in a threat to life or health."

The chairman could feel his authority slipping away. He was desperate to keep control of the meeting before it slipped into complete chaos.

"Councillors, members of the public, please calm down and let me speak. Whilst we would normally ask the planning committee to vote on the proposal in front of them, I feel that we all need more time to consider our position regarding this application. We are aware that this is the second time this proposal has come before us. I am going to ask the council's planning department to reconsider its initial support of this applicant, and also to investigate Mr Packford's claims regarding the possible contamination of the site. I suggest the applicant Viman Developments considers its own position, and if they feel justified, resubmits their proposal with detailed information regarding the cleansing of the site prior to commencement of any building work."

Slowly, calm and order returned to the council chambers and members of the public began to file out. Andy was surrounded by an assortment of people; Harry Thornton was foremost, together with faces he had seen in and around Hollybush Close. Lurking in the background was the newspaper reporter Andy had spoken to previously. Gradually, they left Andy alone. Only Harry and the reporter stayed close.

"Do you want another beer, mate? I'm guessing you might need it after that lot. I'll buy your friend one as well."

The three of them made their way to a nearby pub. Luckily, it was still early and the bar was quite empty. They found a quiet corner and the reporter bought the drinks in.

"Blimey, you certainly know how to get a party going, don't you? You two should form a double act, you're like a bloody tag wrestling team."

Harry was first to respond.

"I don't know anything about planning or building houses or any of that stuff, but I do know I don't like some stuck-up, rich bastard taking the piss out of ordinary folks trying to make a decent life for themselves."

The reporter took a small tape recorder from his pocket.

"Look, fellas, this whole thing is going to get serious. Do you mind if I use this? I don't want to get anything wrong and I don't want to miss anything."

Harry couldn't help but smile.

"Funny, innit. I drive a tipper all day and most people give me and my truck a wide berth. Now, just because I was in the wrong place at the wrong time and saw my mate buried under two tons of gravel, I've become a hero. He died because he was so tired due to his baby crying night after night, and she only cried because of the illness she contracted living in that festering, mould-ridden house that Victor bloody Manning built for them. It makes my blood boil."

Andy added to the conversation.

"It must be something to do with lorries." he joked. "I was a class one driver for a few years before I changed tack and became an antiques dealer. Maybe it's the fact that driving all day gives you plenty of time to think things through, get your priorities straight. Now I'm beginning to sound like an antiques dealer turned building crusader. The fact is, many of the people living in these houses don't have the ability to complain, and if they did, they might find themselves homeless. I am not sure if Harry and I are helping, but I can't stand by and do nothing. It seems to me the whole process is corrupt. Manning buys contaminated land, presumably at a knockdown price; the local council planning department are under pressure to provide more houses, so they pass the plans and turn a blind eye to the contamination, and housing associations are happy to buy anything that will house their waiting tenants. Everyone gains except the people who end up living in substandard houses. Nice, isn't it!"

"Look, this story is going to get bigger. At the moment it's all about a bit of mould on some of the houses and a new development that may get pushed back or worst case, it will be refused. But it concerns a very large and influential building company and possibly corruption at the local council. If it is all a big mistake, it is not too bad; if it's been going on for a long time, it really is going to kick off. Manning will be ruined. and he will not be happy. You guys really do need to mind how you go!" With that, the reporter put away the recorder and got up to leave.

There it was again. Mind how you go.

The reporter left and Andy and Harry were on their own. For the moment at least, they sat in silence, staring into their half-finished beers.

Harry was first to speak.

"What do you reckon? Are we done or is this just the beginning?"

Andy started to smile.

"I don't know about you, Harry, but when I was a kid, my old mum used to say, 'never be afraid to tell the truth'. Well, I wasn't afraid then and I'm not afraid now. I am just going to take it one step at a time. I'm not out for trouble, but I'm not running away from it."

"Andy, that was spoken like a brave man, or an idiot, I'm not sure which. But whatever happens, it looks like we are in it together. I think it would be a good idea if we exchanged phone numbers so that we can stay in touch. Remember, you don't have to do anything alone, just call me. That's all you have to do, mate, just call."

NINETEEN

Manning paced around his office like a caged tiger. Although the office was quite large, he could cover it, wall to wall in ten strides but whichever direction he walked, Seymour was in his way.

"Christ, are you trying to wind me up? Get out of my bloody way! I'm trying to think of a way out of the mess you've got us into."

Seymour reasoned that this was not the right time to remind his boss that the mess was entirely of his own making.

"How much would it cost us to clean the site? Manning asked.

"Well, there would be two costs. One would be financial, about half a million pounds, I would guess and the other would be a time cost. The delay could be as long as six or even twelve months by the time the soil is excavated and dumped, then the site would need to be inspected, then new clean top soil. It could go on and on. And to add to it, all this has already been spread all over the newspapers. We may struggle to attract the buyers."

Manning was silent for several minutes. Seymour stood like a statue, waiting for his reply.

Finally, Manning said, "I'm going to lay off the workforce! I can't afford to pay specialists to clean the site and pay our blokes to sit around waiting six months or more, and we don't have any other sites to put them on. This just gets worse. Leave me alone. I need to think this through before I make any decisions."

Seymour was relieved to get out of Manning's office. For the moment, he still had his job. Right at this moment, he didn't know how long for, or even if he actually wanted it.

The next few days passed normally for Andy and Harry. Harry carried on as usual, collecting sand and gravel in his tipper lorry and delivering it to whatever building site needed it. Some of the other drivers in his depot had seen the reports in the newspaper and given him a bit of a ribbing over it. At home, his wife took a more cautious approach. From past experience, she knew he had a quick temper. something that had landed him in trouble before.

"Harry, please promise me that this thing is not going to get out of hand. I know what you're like. Please don't let it get physical."

"Come on! Why should it get physical? I promise I won't start anything."

"I'm not worried about you starting it, it's you finishing it that bothers me."

Andy tried to carry on as normal. He sold a few nice antiques, enough to pay his wages, and he managed to buy enough to maintain his stock levels. However, he realised he was not entirely comfortable with the new working arrangements he had made with Susan Harrison.

Would she still want to continue the new fledgeling friendship she had started, now that he was so deeply involved in the planning controversy that had serious implications for her husband and their friend Victor Manning? Andy convinced himself that he was not bothered either way. He had been happy before he met her, when she was just another face at the auction. He would be happy to go his own way again without any involvement from her. But maybe he should contact her and ask her. After all, whatever her husband and Manning may or may not have contrived to do, she was not a part of it. He satisfied himself that she probably did not even know.

That's what he would do. Phone her and pretend nothing had happened. If she hung up on him, that would be her answer.

She answered the phone on the second ring. "Hello Andy, I was just going to call you. I have an old table I would like your opinion on. It is a bit distressed now, but I think it will restore quite well. Can I bring it over to you? Maybe you have a few bits and pieces I could take back and put in the shop and sell for you on commission."

Clearly, if there was any resentment on her side, she was good at hiding it.

Twenty minutes later, she was ringing Andy's doorbell with a small, circular coffee table tucked under her arm.

Andy opened the door and let her in. She appeared as bright and friendly as he remembered from their previous meeting, Andy thought maybe she didn't read the newspapers, or maybe her husband never mentioned his work or maybe, like a lot of couples, they never spoke to one another. Either way if she had any issues with him it was not obvious.

He offered her a coffee before they got down to the refurbishment of her old table. She followed him into the small kitchen. He filled the kettle and she took two cups from the mug tree.

"See, the partnership is working well already!" she laughed.

They took their coffee into the lounge and settled onto the sofa. Andy looked at the table she had brought.

"Oh, that shouldn't be any problem to restore. It is actually a nice size, not too big nor too small. Buyers like them like that. When I've finished with it, it will look like new. Well, not quite like new because that would defeat the object of buying an antique table, wouldn't it?"

It wasn't really a joke but they both had a chuckle over his comment.

Andy was still looking over the table, running his hand around the edges to make sure there were no chips or splits. He hadn't looked in Susan's direction since they had sat down but as his arm stretched all the way around, he found himself looking at her, looking at him.

"Look, Susan, there's one thing I have to be clear on. We have had a couple of meetings now and I've really enjoyed them, and if we could work together that would be brilliant. I've changed my opinion of you, and I admire you for building up your business without any help from your husband, but"

Susan interrupted him. "I knew there was going to be a but. It was all going so well until then."

"Please just let me finish. I've got myself involved in the latest planning application by Viman and also the coroner's inquiry into the deaths on one of Viman's estates I'm sure you know about them. Obviously, they involve Manning and

I have a strong feeling that they may involve your husband. If there is going to be any conflict between us, I would like to get it out in the open before we go any further."

She looked him in the eyes.

"My husband was my world. We met when he was at university studying for his degree in town planning. No one was more proud of their man than I was on the day he graduated. Then, when he was promoted to chief planning officer, I was over the moon for him. I had a successful husband and he had the career he'd always wanted. That's when he crossed paths with Manning."

Andy cut in, "I thought you were one of Manning's supporters. Gladiatorial spirit and all that. That is what you said about his motor racing."

"Yes. I know, I did say that. And in the beginning I truly felt that about him but I quickly realised that Manning was just using my husband to further his own ends. Joining him for his winner's hospitality at the race track was a crumb of the high life he threw us. Although I was thrilled by the excitement, I was horrified at what Manning and my husband had become. Ever the loyal wife, I played along and believe me, I mean it, you are the only person I've spoken to like this. No one else knows the truth. I put a brave face on for the public and always say the right things, but I despise my husband for what he has become, what Manning has made him. I have no love left for him now. Ours is a loveless marriage. It has been for a long time. So, if you must expose him and some of the things he's done, frankly, he deserves it."

Andy was taken by surprise, both by what she had said and how she had said it. She was dry eyed, no sign of tears. If there had been tears, they must have been a long while ago.

She looked at him and curled her lips into a small, almost coy smile and gently shrugged her shoulders as if to say, 'I know you didn't expect that, but it's the truth.'

For once, Andy was lost for words. He sat there staring at her. It was one of those moments when time stands still and a few seconds, not even a few seconds, fractions of a second seem like hours. He slowly raised his arms and placed his hands on her shoulders. Together, in what appeared to be choreographed slow motion, their lips moved closer and closer until they were locked in a passionate kiss. They could not help themselves. Time stood still for that first embrace. How long did it last? Minutes, hours, days even. That is how it seemed to them. In real time, maybe it lasted ten seconds, maybe twenty seconds, but for the two of them on that day, it lasted forever.

Andy was first to speak. "I didn't mean for that to happen. You just seemed so alone, so vulnerable, like a lost little girl. I'm sorry if.."

She raised her finger to stop him.

"Please don't be sorry. You have nothing to apologise for. I knew it would happen, I didn't know when or where, but I knew it would happen. I have known it since I first saw you. The question is what happens now?"

The question was never answered. The air was filled with the sound of a shrieking car alarm. Andy jumped to his feet.

"I think that's my BMW alarm."

He ran out of the flat to find his old estate car with the hazard lights flashing and the alarm wailing like a banshee. As he ran closer, he failed to see the two men standing to one side, partly hidden from view by an old van.

He walked around the car, checking the doors and windows for any sign of a break in.

Two figures walked out from the shadow of the parked van and towards him.

"Was this anything to do with you two? Were you trying to steal my car?"

"You're joking, mate, who would want to steal this pile of old junk? Now, we have your attention, we'd like to ask you a question. What would you do if some nosey bastard tried to stop you working? You know, stopped you earning. 'Cos that's what you've done to us. Thanks to your interfering, we're out of work. You and your mate have stopped Viman getting their new site going and as a result he's laid us off. I'll tell you what you are going to do. Nothing. That's what you're going to do. Don't turn up for the next planning meeting. don't go to the coroner's court and don't say nothing to the papers. Get it?"

Andy stood his ground. While they were threatening him, he was planning his next move. Option one was to walk away and laugh at them. Option two was to try and explain the planning procedure to these two neanderthals and show them that their boss's actions were responsible for them losing their jobs. He chose option three.

"Look guys, this is how I see it. I caught you trying to break into my car. The whole block of flats heard the alarm going. I would be well within my rights to try to stop you. Are you still with me? Maybe in the struggle one of you might end up with a broken arm or broken fingers. How could you lay bricks or dig holes or whatever you do in that state? I don't want any trouble. You can walk away or I will put one of you in the hospital. Your choice."

Clearly they weren't expecting that sort of response. Both men looked older than Andy and both looked a lot heavier and both definitely had beer bellies. After a quick glance at one another, they both moved towards him.

He had already decided he would take the larger one first. It was unlikely a second, smaller man will chance his arm if his larger accomplice is screaming in agony.

Andy's target was on his left as they approached him. When he was five feet away, Andy moved quickly left and forward, bringing him level with his assailant. In an instant, Andy stamped his right foot into the man's knee. As his body bent forward clutching his broken kneecap, Andy used both hands to take two gnarled builder's fingers in each hand. One quick snatch and he had four broken fingers to add to the broken knee. Target one was out of commission and suddenly target two looked a lot less enthusiastic.

"You bastard! You haven't heard the last of this."

"Oh, I think I have. My neighbour there has got this recorded on her phone. Two big builders threatening one unassuming, peaceful antiques dealer when he found them stealing his car."

The smaller builder helped the other into the van and they drove off. Andy returned to his flat to find Susan distraught.

"I really thought you were in trouble then. I was terrified."

"I'm sorry you had to see that. As we are both revealing our secrets, I'm sorry to say that was one of mine. Before I settled down, I mixed with some rough kids and I learnt how to look after myself. It didn't take me long to realise that if you can walk away from trouble, you should do it. If you can't, sort it quickly while you have the chance. I figured those two were out for blood, they saw me as the bad guy and thought they could scare me off. If they had spent more time at the gym and less in the pub, they might have done. As it is, by the time he's recovered, Manning might have something for him to build."

"Please, Andy, don't joke about it, that could have been serious. Is there anything else I should know? Let's be honest with each other and get our secrets out in the open."

"No, that's it. Actually, as a teenager I was a bit of an athlete. I was a keen cyclist, my club champion, then after all the training and dedication I went off the rails for a short while and as I said, mixed with the wrong crowd. But I quickly realised I was heading down a one-way street and changed my life around. I became a lorry driver and I loved it to begin with, but after my marriage broke up I decided to become an antiques dealer and basically that's it."

"You dressed in tight-fitting Lycra. That's something I would love to see!"

They looked at each other and couldn't stop themselves bursting into a fit of giggles.

"Andy, I came here today hoping our new friendship might develop into something a little deeper. I had no idea which way I wanted it to go, just a little deeper. Now I have found something with you that I haven't experienced in my life for a long, long time. I'm not explaining this very well, I don't even know if it makes any sense, but I can talk to you in a way I haven't spoken to anyone before."

Andy realised that he had also turned a corner in his life, and it frightened him. Susan was a lot older than him and she was Mrs Harrison, and Mr Harrison was still very much alive. Together they would have led a different life to the one he could offer her. Would there be any future for their new relationship? Were they in fact embarking on a relationship?

He held her close, "Look, Susan, I do enjoy your company, much more than I thought I could, but I don't want our friendship to be based on false promises. I don't know if I can promise you happiness in the future, or even if we have a future. I suppose what I am trying to say is, that, like you, I don't want this to end but I don't know what direction it might take us. Let's take each step as it comes. Deal?"

"Deal." she said.

He enveloped her in his arms and they savoured the moment. Whatever the future held, they vowed they would face it together.

TWENTY

The following two weeks Andy spent more and more of his time with Susan. Their plans to work together, Andy restoring her furniture and Susan selling his antiques, proved both profitable and pleasurable for them. They both found a new happiness in their lives. Any thoughts of the simmering conflict with Victor Manning or the planning department were pushed to the back of their minds.

Andy's newfound peace and happiness was disturbed by the postman. He received a letter from the coroner's office requesting his presence at the reconvened inquiry into the deaths of the Jones family.

He had been expecting it. He had been one of the more vocal witnesses and it was inevitable that he would be called back to present his evidence.

He never regarded himself as an expert, he never thought of himself as a crusader for justice; he did, however, think of himself as a voice for those who could not speak for themselves.

He knew that this latest inquiry would be more searching and he promised himself that unlike before, when he had spoken on the spur of the moment, this time he would be prepared.

He called Harry Thornton and found that he had also been summoned to attend the inquest. While they were discussing the roles they would play and the evidence they would give, Andy told him about the fracas with Viman's two builders.

"You sound like you can handle yourself, but you really need to take care. Some of these guys can play pretty rough. One or two might be okaybut if they come at you mob handed you might need an escape plan, if you get my drift."

"Yeah, I take your point Harry. I've made a policy of not looking for trouble but if it comes my way I'm not running. I can't change my personality overnight. But you are right, I'll try and work out a plan B, that way I'm covered for whatever might happen. Between you and me, Harry, I am more concerned about what I'm going to say to the inquest. I want to get my point over but I don't want to get too bogged down with technical stuff and the names of pollutants that I can't really pronounce or fully understand. I'm a lorry driver turned antiques dealer not a scientist. I have to sit down and think very carefully about what I'm going to say. How about you?"

"Oh! I am okay. I've collected sand and gravel at loads of different pits. Like you, I'm not an expert but I have a fair idea of what looks right and what doesn't. And what they had to do and the machinery they had to do it with at Holdstock was just way out of order. That's what I'm going to tell the coroner."

"Fair enough, Harry. I'll see you in court, as they say!"

With that, Andy hung up the phone and settled into a chair. He needed to clear his mind and plan what he was going to say to the coroner. In his mind he went over the facts as he saw them. The houses in Hollybush Close all suffered from some form of fungus and mould. The larger houses at the top of the estate seemed to be okay and free of mould. But the houses in Hollybush Close were built quite a bit lower maybe the contaminated chemicals left behind when the plating works closed had somehow permeated the lower soil and left the higher land untouched. Whatever the reason, the mould had infected Jessica with something that had caused her illness and ultimately contributed to her death. He remembered his conversation with Mrs Wilkins, the elderly lady who lived behind the new estate. She had mentioned that her husband had died after years of working at the plating works. Maybe this was a better way to explain the dangers involved in the processes and the chemicals that were used on the site before it became a housing estate.

Andy parked his car outside the small terraced house. As he walked up the narrow path to the front door, he was aware that Mrs Wilkins was peering through her curtains at the stranger coming to her house. Before he had time to use the large heavy door knocker, he heard her call out, "Who's there? What do you want?"

"Mrs Wilkins, I spoke to you a few weeks ago, do you remember? About the old plating works and your husband's unfortunate death."

The coroner's court was part of a larger building that contained some of the more obscure council departments. Andy parked his BMW in the car park at the rear. As he walked to the pay machine for a ticket, he saw Harry Thornton arrive. Andy waited for him to park and together they walked to the nearest ticket dispenser, chatting as they went about the imminent inquiry. The machine they were heading for was in the corner of the car park. As they squeezed between two parked cars, one of the driver's doors swung open behind them, momentarily knocking Harry off his feet.

The driver climbed out followed by two others who were in the back seat.

"This is handy boys, we've got both of the interfering, nosey bastards together. Now we've got two jobs here. One is to make you pay for what you did to our mate, the other is to remind you to keep your mouth zipped."

Harry was quickly up and on his feet. "Listen, fellas "he said. "We are only doing what any decent working man would do. By his greed your boss either knowingly or by neglect killed a baby girl. That is bad enough but her sickness resulted in her father losing his life and the mother, bless her, couldn't carry on alone so she killed herself. All so your boss could keep his millions and go bloody motor racing. Now does that seem fair to you? Is it worth fighting for? My mate Andy and me have no quarrel with you guys but by God, we both think those three dead people are worth fighting for. So, if that is what you want, then come on, then."

The three builders were in no mood to back down. For years they had made a good living building whatever Victor Manning told them to. Now they were laid off, in their minds by the actions of the two men in front of them.

The gap between the parked cars was only a door's width, probably no more than a metre so only wide enough for one man to stand across it. Harry stood in the gap level with the front of the parked car, Andy stood to his right, between the front of their car and the rear of the car in the next row.

The builder took three paces towards Harry and swung a right hook. Harry saw it coming and made a small step backward. He used the momentum of the hook to spin his attacker around so that in the small gap he was off balance and ended sprawled over the bonnet of his own car.

Harry moved closer and kicked his feet away so the whole force of the swing and his body weight was directed through his face onto the bonnet.

While Harry was dealing with the first builder, Andy quickly ran down the other side of the car to come up behind the other two. A sharp kick behind the knee sent the nearest of them stumbling forward into the third one. With nowhere to go and no room to turn around, two attackers were bundled up on the ground whilst the third was still making a close inspection of the car bonnet.

Before the attackers could regain their balance and composure, Andy reached through the open car window and snatched out the ignition keys. Standing a few feet in front of them, with the keys dangling on his finger, Andy confronted their apparent leader.

"Listen, fellas, we can try and knock seven bells out of each other for as long as you like but it won't change the situation. Your boss Victor Manning has been building houses that are not fit for purpose. To put it in plain English, residents are getting ill and dying. Fair enough, we understand that he has laid you off and you are not earning any money, but that's down to him, not us. Whether you like it or not, he is responsible for the deaths in that family and if we can, Harry and me will try and stop him building on any similarly dangerous sites. Look at it like this, would you like your kids to live in a mouldering, festering house? Now, do you want to call a truce to this and get your car keys back or are we going into round two, which will start with me throwing your keys away? Your choice."

"Okay, you know we didn't have anything to do with those deaths. We only work where he tells us. But if you are right, it's not proper that anyone should live in those conditions. Me and the rest of the boys have our own kids and we would fight tooth and nail to protect them. Look, no hard feelings. You do what you have to do and we'll hope that Manning can come up with something soon."

Andy tossed the car keys back and he and Harry walked out of the car park towards the coroner's court.

The coroner opened the inquiry and said that he intended to deal with the death of Graham Jones first. He called Harry Thornton.

"Mr Thornton, I understand you actually witnessed the tragic accident. In your own words, can you describe what happened?"

"Well, Sir, I arrived at Holdstock Quarry as normal. I parked the lorry in the usual position, waiting to be loaded. As usual I sat in the cab. I could see the arms of the shovel in my rear-view mirror. That's when things started to go wrong. I knew that the shovel hadn't opened because I didn't feel the load landing in the truck. Well, to be honest, it wasn't really a case of things going wrong because at this quarry the shovel very rarely opened without any problems. I didn't see the operator, Mr Jones, climb onto my lorry because he was out of my sight line. So, I got out of the cab in time to see him standing in the back of the truck. He shouted that the bucket had jammed again and he was in the process of trying to free it."

The coroner interrupted Harry. "Mr Thornton, you say this is a regular occurrence. How often would the bucket jam?"

"I would say that it jammed at least once every time my wagon was loaded. Sometimes when Mr Jones and me had a tea break together, he would tell me about his boss at the quarry and how he would save money by not getting the machinery serviced properly. Mr Jones was having problems at home with his daughter being ill and all and I think he was trying to work faster to make up for lost time. To be honest, I felt sorry for him. If he didn't resort to hitting the bucket when it jammed, he wouldn't get any work done and then the boss would be on his back to speed things up. He couldn't win either way."

"Thank you, Mr Thornton. I now have a clear picture of what happened." The coroner then called Sergeant Grove. "Sergeant, in your own words, will you please describe what you saw when you arrived at Holdstock Quarry?"

"Yes, Sir. When I arrived, the ambulance was just leaving with the injured man. Everyone was in an excited state; many of the men were covered in dirt and had bleeding hands and fingers. I formed the opinion that there had been some sort of accident and that they had been trying to dig him out with their bare hands. The quarry manager, Mr Ashton, introduced himself to me but it was obvious that the men thought him responsible for what had happened. For his own safety I took him into custody and later I believe he made a statement to the health and safety inspector."

The coroner interrupted, "Yes, I have a copy of that statement here. Thank you, Sergeant Grove. You may return to your seat."

The inquest continued with evidence from the health and safety inspector. He confirmed that the service log for the machinery was up to date, but he also said,what all those who worked at Holdstock knew very well, that the work was not carried out by a competent mechanic with the necessary training or experience. In short, there was no way of knowing what service or repair work had been carried out, if any.

George Ashton was next to give evidence. He maintained that he had full confidence in the mechanic he used and he had no reason to question his ability to work on the machinery. He insisted that all the workforce had regular health and safety briefings and they were all aware of their own obligations regarding personal safety.

After hearing all the evidence, the coroner arrived at his decision. Graham Jones had died as a result of miss-adventure. Although the working practices at Holdstock Quarry fell well below those expected at such a workplace, Graham Jones had placed himself in a dangerous position which had in turn contributed to his death.

The coroner then considered the death of baby Jessica Jones. First to give evidence was the doctor who had attended to Jessica in the hospital. He explained that the actual cause of death was pneumonia brought on by chronic lung infection. In his capacity as a doctor, he felt unqualified to give an explanation as to what had caused the infection but whatever the cause he felt sure that she had been suffering for some considerable time. To the extent that by the time she was admitted to hospital, she was beyond their help.

Next to be called to present their evidence was Andrew Packford.

"You may recall, Sir, that at the earlier inquest I presented details of the former use of this site, which, in my opinion, contributed to the mould and fungus that is present in many of the houses. You may also recall that I spoke to Mrs Wilkins. After that first inquiry, I spoke with her again. Her house is on one of the roads that runs behind the new site and as such overlooks the new houses. In layman's terms, she described to me how she could sit in her kitchen and watch the construction work on the Viman's site. Whilst she knows nothing about building practices or methods, she is very clear in what she saw. As her late husband worked at the plating factory, she was aware that the whole area was awash with corrosive chemicals, particularly the area around Hollybush Close, which is the lowest part of the whole site. And whilst she observed the construction work on a regular basis, she was certain that she did not see any lorries taking away the contaminated topsoil. All the lorries she saw were delivering, not removing. It was common knowledge amongst the local residents that the chemicals used in the various plating processes had, over time, eroded the structure of the original buildings, which in turn had forced the owners to abandon the business. It is my opinion that the chemicals were still present in the soil and that they leaked up into the structure of the new houses and ultimately killed Jessica Jones. Thank you, Sir, for giving me the opportunity to present the facts to this inquiry."

"Thank you, Mr Packford. You have clearly gone to a lot of trouble to provide this inquiry with facts that otherwise might not have been heard."

The last witness the Coroner called was Mark Seymour.

"Mr Seymour, you are the senior planning officer at Viman Developments. Is that correct?"

"Yes, Sir". Seymour replied somewhat sheepishly. At this moment, he would rather he was the office cleaner. He knew he was in for a rough ride.

"Mr Seymour, can you explain to me the procedure for establishing if a particular plot of land is suitable for building on?"

"Yes, Sir, of course." Seymour replied slowly, giving himself time to think about what he was going to say next.

"It is the local council's responsibility to keep a register of all contaminated land. In this instance, there was no such record of this site being at risk. We tested the land for signs of contamination and the tests came back negative. We then tested to establish what foundations were necessary and in due course we commenced construction, all in accordance and in conjunction with the council's own planning and design department."

"Mr Seymour." the coroner interrupted, "Are you sure that there were no indications that this land was contaminated?"

"Yes Sir. All our tests proved negative. We had no reason not to build."

Andy Packford slowly rose to his feet. "I'm sorry if this is a breach of protocol but I think it is important for all the people involved, we need to know where on the site the tests were carried out."

"Mr Packford." The coroner snapped back, "Your evidence has been quite informative but your question is a severe breach of court etiquette. In case you haven't realised, I ask the questions. Please remain seated and quiet! However, you have raised a crucial point. Please tell us, Mr Seymour, whereabouts on this large site you conducted your contamination survey."

Seymour looked more than a little flustered. "When we first visited the site there were a lot of old disused buildings, many of which were in such a bad state of repair that it would have been dangerous for anyone to enter them. So, with regard to safety, all our tests were carried out close to the entrance to the old factory."

"And what would that area have been used for when the plating works were operative?" the coroner asked.

Now showing serious signs of pressure, Seymour replied in a whisper, "Er, I think it was the old car park area."

Andy Packford, Harry Thornton and all the public gallery knew Seymour was on the ropes.

The coroner sensed that he was now getting the facts he needed.

"Am I right in assuming that the area you tested would eventually be where the large houses were built, the houses that are not affected by the contamination and that the lower part of the site, where the actual plating factory had stood and which would subsequently be the position of the social houses remained untested?"

Seymour was now sweating and looking down, seemingly checking his fingernails.

"Ye..yes, Sir, I think that would be correct."

"You may sit down, Mr Seymour." The coroner ordered.

A buzz had gone around the packed courtroom. Everyone knew it was over, the truth had finally been dragged out of Viman Developments. Unfortunately, Victor Manning wasn't there to hear the coroner's verdict. But he would know all about it very shortly.

The coroner addressed the courtroom.

"My verdict is that Jessica Jones died as a result of

negligence by the construction firm that built the house she lived in. With regard to Alison Jones, I find that she took her own life while the balance of her mind was disturbed. I would just like to put on record that, although these three deaths occurred in different circumstances and different locations, they were all linked and indeed, the responsibility must lie with the construction company and to some extent the local council and their building inspectors, who oversaw the work."

The silence in the courtroom lasted a full five seconds, that's how long it took for the final verdict to register with all those who heard it. Then it exploded in a mixture of cheering and clapping. People in the public gallery rose from their seats to congratulate Andy. He felt dozens of grateful hands slapping him on his back or trying to shake his hand. But the memory he would take away from the day was the tear stained face of the young mum who lived next door to the Jones', the neighbour who had invited him in and made him a cup of tea.

"I still don't know who you are or why you would want to help us but I do know all this would have been swept under the carpet if you hadn't got involved. Maybe now the authorities will take notice and condemn these evil houses. And maybe we will get somewhere decent to live. All I can say is thank you, Andrew Packford."

As he left the building, Andy caught up with Harry Thornton, "I don't know about you, Harry, but I'm glad that's over. Perhaps things can get back to normal now. If there are any further enquiries or whatever then someone else can get involved. At least you and I have lifted the lid on this and now everyone will know what went on."

"Yeah, I'll drink to that." Harry said as they walked towards their cars. Then he added, "Let's hope our cars are still in one piece after our earlier encounter."

"Oh, I think we've heard the last of the tough guy builders." Andy replied. "At the end of the day, they're not thugs. They're just like you and me trying to make a living the only way they know how. Come to think of it, that's all the Joneses wanted. You know, I never really intended to get involved with this, but now I have and hopefully it's over, I'm glad that I made the effort. I would blame myself forever if I'd stood by and done nothing. And Harry, I was grateful to know that you were with me."

For once Harry was lost for words.

"Oh, cut it out will you? we were just two blokes doing what decent blokes should do."

On his way home from the coroner's court, Andy stopped off at Susan's shop. As he entered, she was explaining the merits of a mahogany side table to an eagerly listening customer. She skilfully explained that yes, it had been restored to a point that it could be used and enjoyed to the full, but definitely not over restored, it still looked like the antique it was. As she talked other customers were trying to catch bits of the conversation as they looked around the small, rather crowded shop. Andy was still buzzing from the earlier excitement and in no mood to stand idly by. Walking up to a browsing customer, he introduced himself.

"Hello, I'm Andy, Susan's partner. Do you need any help?" He knew that a polite, light conversation would be an ice breaker, so he continued, "Yes, madam, the item you're looking at is solid silver. Look, here are the hallmarks. They tell when it was made, where it was made and who made it.

So, this snuff box is one hundred and forty years old. Just think of the stories it could tell. And the best part of owning something like this is that you can enjoy it and then pass it on down through your family and the very best part is, that in twenty- or thirty-years time, it will be worth twice what it's worth now. There aren't many things you can buy nowadays for one hundred and eighty pounds that will do that."

For the second time that day, Andy had made a difference. Susan had closed the sale on the table and was standing behind the counter, ready to take the customer's cash for the snuff box. After the customers had left, she turned to Andy.

"It's a good job you came when you did, I could sense that particular customer was about to leave. I was so tied up with the lady over the table. Sorry. Sorry. I am going on about me. What about you? I had forgotten about your coroner's inquest. How did it go?"

"Well, it was just another boring day really, Harry and I had a scuffle with three angry builders, I managed to upset the decorum of the courtroom and got told off by the coroner but Susan, we did it. We made everyone aware that Viman Developments and Victor Manning are building houses that are not fit for purpose. I am not sure if it might implicate your husband, I suspect it might and it might possibly ruin Manning, but frankly, they had it coming."

"Andy, please don't make light of these things. You could have got hurt and I would hate that. I've told you, I'm not interested in what might happen to my husband, our marriage is over, our life together is over. I didn't intend to drop this on you now, but do you think we could be more than business partners? I mean much more."

"Susan, are you sure you know what you are saying? I can't promise you anything. I live in a tiny flat, I drive a knackered old car and I don't have any money. But if it's possible to share nothing, there is no one I'd rather share it with than you."

"Andrew Packford, that is the most romantic thing anyone has ever said to me. I am closing the shop early today. No, *we're* closing *our* shop early today. Please take me back to your tiny flat but stop on the way so I can buy a new toothbrush."

They both collapsed into a fit of giggles.

The next few weeks raced by. Most days, Susan worked at the shop and Andy worked in his garage, restoring everything from tables and chairs to well-worn pieces of silver. Except, of course, on Fridays when they both went to Miller and Jackman Fine Arts auctioneers.

TWENTY-ONE

Angela looked her usual elegant self. Business like but not too severe, desirable but not brassy. In fact, she had a knack of looking just right.

"Good morning, Mr Manning." She said as she walked into his office. The greeting was more for the benefit of the outer office staff who might be listening than Manning himself. "There is one letter in the day's mail that is addressed to you personally and it was sent recorded delivery. Everything else I've taken to the relevant departments."

Manning didn't say anything, he just took the letter from her. As was his usual practice, he sat well back in his chair and held out his hand. He held it out, he didn't stretch it out which meant she had to reach over the desk, which gave him time to look down the top of her blouse. It was no big deal, he did it most days. Being the object of his lustful gaze was easy compared with some of the things she had to do.

By the time Angela had turned and reached the door, Manning had opened the envelope and read at least some of the contents.

"Bloody bastards! They can't do that. Do they know what they've started?"

Angela didn't know whether she should walk out or try to placate her boss. She continued walking, quietly closing the door behind her.

At Telcote Manor, Howard Fryer was checking and fine tuning the Ford Mustang. Manning's next race was not for another four weeks but it was at the Spa circuit in Belgium. Fryer knew it was one of the fastest tracks and the type of race that would be won by the car with the most power, plain and simple. No ifs, no buts, just brute force.

Manning had always allowed his team of mechanics a free hand and an open cheque book to maintain his car to the highest possible standards. He knew Fryer was an expert and he left the preparation of the car to him. Anything he needed was available. For Spa, the Mustang would have a different computerised engine management system along with modified brakes. The size of the brake discs would be increased, also the balance of the brakes. As with most racing cars, the brake balance could be adjusted by the driver during the race, changing the ratio of front or rear wheel braking. In addition, the cooling airflow to the brakes would be improved to eliminate overheating and brake fade. Maximum speed and the ability to stop would be the priorities. When the work was finished, Fryer would enter all the changes into the car's race log and present a copy directly to Manning in case he wanted to veto anything. This was just a formality as Fryer could not remember an occasion when Manning had not been happy with the work the team had done.

Victor Manning had already read the letter three times. Now he was reading it again, trying to absorb the contents, trying to slow down his racing heart and his rising anger.

"Dear Sir,

I am instructed by my clients, Glendown Housing Association Ltd, to inform you that following the recent unfortunate incidents at Hollybush Close and the findings of the subsequent coroner's inquest, my client intends to pursue Viman Developments for the return of the money they previously paid for twelve properties situated on Hollybush Close. In addition, they seek reimbursement for extra costs involved in rehoming the families living in said houses. At the time of writing, the total costs have not been finalised but they are expected to be in the region of three million pounds sterling, plus any expenses incurred in obtaining a settlement. My clients have suggested that as a goodwill gesture they would be happy to accept an interim payment of two million pounds while they arrive at a final figure.

Yours faithfully
John L. Francis
Francis James and Francis Solicitors."

Manning tried to compose himself. It's not as if this was the first time he had received a solicitor's letter. He considered the options. He could ignore it, but it was unlikely to go away and would eventually be made public, which could ruin him.

He could pay, which would ruin him financially and would definitely become public. He could try and turn the issue around and maybe he might come out the other side to look like a good guy.

He called Mark Seymour into his office.

"Get a firm price for clearing the contamination on the foundry site. Do not cut any corners.Get a reputable firm with a good proven history in that type of thing. Get it all sewn up tight, all on paper, all above board. Tie them down to an early start and a fast completion. Do not sign anything until you have run it past me. Did you get all that?"

"Yes, no problem, Mr Manning. I'll get it all sorted and, on your desk, as soon as I can."

With that, Seymour left the office feeling slightly more confident about his long-term job prospects.

Manning asked Angela to get his solicitor on the phone. When he came through, Manning read him the letter he had received and outlined the response he intended to make.

"Victor, I don't see anything fundamentally wrong with what you propose but be careful. No admission of guilt and nothing in writing that you cannot back up."

That was all the assurance Manning needed.Next, he called Derek Harrison.

"Listen, I'm going to get the foundry site cleared. Yes. Cleared of all the contamination. Yes, by a specialist approved contractor. How quickly can you get the planning permission through? Okay, so if I get it cleared within the next month I could be on site and building in two months. If I do my bit, make bloody sure you do yours. I can't afford for this to go tits up again. Okay Derek. Look, I am sorry but I'm in a bit of a spot at the moment. Nothing I can't sort but

I could do without it. How are things with you? How is that lovely wife of yours? She's what! Playing around with some young antiques dealer? Say, it's not the same nosey bastard who's been sticking his beak into my houses? Bloody hell, you reckon it is him? She will soon get fed up with him. I can't believe he can afford to keep her in the style that she deserves, then she'll come running back, all tears and regrets. Bloody women! I don't know who this bloke is but he's beginning to seriously piss me off. Alright Derek, I will talk to you soon. Cheers."

Manning called Angela into his office.

"Take down this reply to these solicitors please, Angela." He said, waving the letter. "Dear Sir, I understand your client's concern regarding the houses on Hollybush Close, however I am mystified as to the cause of the apparent fungus and mould. I appreciate the coroner's comments but until a detailed examination is carried out by environmental experts, it would be unwise to jump to any hasty conclusions. I think we all agree that the most important thing at the moment is to rehome the unfortunate families as soon as possible. To that end, I am happy to tell you that Viman Developments will very shortly be commencing work on a new housing estate. As an appreciation of the goodwill that exists between my company and your client, I am happy to cancel the sale of the affected homes and to offer replacement houses on the new development. To emphasise our commitment, I am prepared to offer your client a further three houses completely free of charge. I have also enclosed a cheque to the value of ten thousand pounds to help your client with any immediate expenses. I feel sure that you and your client will understand that Viman Developments is doing everything we possibly can to find a mutually acceptable solution to this disturbing situation. On receipt of your acceptance, I will instruct our solicitors to organise the necessary contracts. Yours etc."

Angela closed her notebook and looked across at her boss. It had been a long time since she had seen him like this. In recent years, he had the air of a man who had everything he wanted, ruthless but at the same time content, even smug. But now she saw a different side of him. He was scheming, almost grovelling, but at the same time fighting to keep his company and his name intact.

She rarely made any comment to him about the business, she knew only too well that he didn't employ her for her opinions but as she turned to leave, she said, "I'll have this typed up for you straight away. If you don't mind me saying, I know things have been awkward for the company lately but I think this could be the turning point. That is a very generous offer to make. I'm sure they will accept."

"Thanks, Angela. I hope you are right. Before you type the letter, get our site manager on the phone for me. He's probably sitting at home twiddling his thumbs after I laid him off."

Angela put the call through.

"Hello, Ray. Are you fed up with sitting at home watching afternoon television? Good. I've got some work for you and your boys."

Andy and Susan's new partnership blossomed and developed in ways they never thought possible. They both realised that to some onlookers, the age gap between them might appear unusual, even unhealthy. But to them it did not exist. Why would it? They were two people who shared the same

111

interests, two people who had lost their first loves, both, ironically, due to pressures created by work, in Andy's case, the long unsociable hours of a lorry driver and in Susan's case the unending ambitions of her husband. Now, as love has given them a second chance, they were both determined to hold on to the opportunity they had been given.

They were free of the confines of a structured existence. They could work as hard as they wanted and if they chose to take things a little easier, they could. Life could not get much better. So long as their growing business produced enough money to live on and so long as they were left alone, they were living the dream. The days rolled along. Generally, Susan worked in the shop while Andy cleaned and restored the antiques they sold.

Susan found qualities in Andy that she never knew existed in men. He treated her as his equal, as indeed she was. Someone to talk to, someone to laugh with and, if the situation should ever arise, someone to cry with. They were partners. Partners in every sense of the word. In the business, in the shop, about the apartment and in the bedroom. Susan found an attentive lover, eager but never pushy, sympathetic but never demanding and much more importantly, always there.

For Andy, Susan provided the anchor that had been missing in his life for so long. Always at his side, always listening to him, occasionally disagreeing with him but still listening. More importantly, they listened to each other.

Ray Stone had worked for Viman for fifteen years, starting as a carpenter and working his way up to site manager. It had been hard work. Sometimes he wondered if it was really worth it. As a carpenter he had done as he was told. So long as he worked to schedule and didn't cause any hold-ups or start any disputes Viman Developments were happy to overlook the odd time saving shortcut, the extra spacings between roof joists, meaning that if he was lucky, he could fix one less joist, extra spacings between nails, and so it went on. Anything to make the job faster and cheaper. The arrangement suited everyone.

As site manager, he was expected to ensure that all the tradesmen cut corners, just as long as the customer, the poor mug who would be paying for the house over the next twenty-five years, didn't find out.

There wasn't much chance of that. How much did the average buyer know about building? So long as the kitchen cupboards looked good and so long as there were no leaks, everyone was happy. And how did Victor Manning reward such loyal, if misguided, service? By laying him off when work was scarce. Nice!

Now Manning had sent him and his men to clean up these filthy, fungus-stained houses. His instructions were to get rid of all the signs of fungus and make the houses look acceptable so that they could be resold to new buyers. But do not spend too much on new materials! They had been working for two weeks in the overpowering stench of damp and decay, tearing out sheets of rotten plasterboard. Black and stained on the surfaces that once formed the lounge wall but the mould that was hidden from sight behind the sheets made even the strongest stomachs heave. Living growths of disease. Several inches of thick, oozing black slime. Two of his gang were already coughing uncontrollably. Unable to get their breath, they spent more time gasping and wheezing than they did working. Ray questioned why, after fifteen years of faithful service, Manning would treat him like this, firstly, laying him off without any notice and then sending him to work on these death trap houses.

Ray knew that these properties needed more than just a quick makeover, they needed pulling down. And soon.

Since the coroner's inquest into the deaths of the Jones family, the activities of Viman Developments had become a regular feature in the local newspaper. The preliminary inquest, followed by the adjourned planning application and then the resumed inquest had been well chronicled, including the evidence given by Andy and Harry Thornton. Neither of them considered themselves as crusaders but they had both received a certain amount of admiration from the readers of the newspaper. Of course, that admiration was not shared by Victor Manning.

The latest edition of the paper covered the story of Viman's offer to rehome the affected families in new houses. It went on to say how the original houses were being refurbished and left it to the reader to guess that once the work was completed, they would be sold to unsuspecting new buyers, no doubt at the market price relevant at that time.

Andy had read most of the articles. What Manning was doing did not concern him too much. The way he saw things, selling a home to a private buyer who had every opportunity to check the property before he signed on the line was one thing. After all, he was an antiques dealer and he was aware of the expression 'buyer beware'. But passing off badly built homes to a housing association for an unsuspecting family to occupy was something else.

Ray Stone turned to the two workmen.

"The ambulance will be here in a few minutes, boys. They'll soon get you right."

The men were in no position to offer any reply. All morning they had coughed and gasped and generally fought for every breath. Now they were collapsed and fighting for life.

He tried to sound reassuring and convincing, but he knew they were empty words. In truth he didn't know what was wrong with them, but he knew it was connected to these damned houses.

As if talking to himself he added, "I suppose I better phone the boss, the bastard."

"I know you want the houses cleaned up as soon as possible but I can't do it if my men are in hospital. If you want my opinion, boss, the whole lot needs to be bulldozed into the ground."

"Ray, I don't want your opinion. I just want you to do as I have told you. Do you know how much this has cost me? If you can't do the job, I'll get someone who can."

"Fine, get someone else to do your dirty work. I've had enough! Fifteen years I've put up with you and your shortcuts and all the dodgy deals. I hope to God that these guys pull through but from what I've seen this morning, I'm not so sure. Now I've got to go to their homes and tell their families what's happened."

Victor Manning never heard Ray's last words. He had already thrown the phone down. He poured himself a drink and tried to calm down. But as he held the glass, he realised his hand was shaking. It was still shaking when Angela buzzed the intercom.

"I've got Howard on the phone, will you take the call?"

"Yeah, put him through."

"Just a reminder, Mr Manning. The car's been ready now for a few days, everything is set for Spa. I wondered if you wanted to test it before we finalised things?"

"Yeah, good idea, Howard. Sorry, I've been a bit busy lately. A day testing would be a bit of a relief after the day I've had. Can you fix it up for me? How about Silverstone tomorrow?"

"I'm sure that will be okay. I'll get it sorted and see you there in the morning."

"Thanks. I'll see you there." The phone call had helped Manning to settle down. No one was listening as he muttered, "At least something is going right. It bloody well should do for the money it costs."

TWENTY-TWO

Howard Fryer and his team of mechanics arrived at the race circuit before their boss. They were there long enough to unload the transporter and give the Mustang a final safety check before starting the engine. When Victor Manning arrived, Fryer was sitting in the racing seat and gently blipping the accelerator, warming the engine and transmission oils.

Manning changed into his racing overalls and swapped places with the mechanic. Over the deafening noise of the V8 engine, Fryer explained the alterations he had carried out during the past weeks. For his part, Manning just wanted to get going, a chance to clear his head and forget the problems he had temporarily left behind in his office.

Most of Fryer's advice fell on deaf ears.

There were a few other cars on the circuit, mainly local club racers driving various modified saloons, trying to race on a shoestring; definitely not in the same league as Manning with his impressive transporter and team of mechanics. He joined the circuit and threaded his way through the smaller and slower cars, taking things relatively easy until the engine, tyres and brakes reached their respective operating temperatures.

After six laps, the rasping exhaust note of the big V8 engine changed to a higher, busier rumble as the driver increased the engine revs and the car dramatically increased speed. The first full power lap had the mechanics checking their stopwatches. Manning may have business problems but his performance on the track gave no indication that he had other things on his mind. He was getting very close to the historic sports car lap record.

Fryer knew it was his job to provide his employer with the fastest car possible, but Manning's driving was making him nervous. This was supposed to be a pre-race shakedown, not a display of unnecessary bravado.

"Let's bring him in and let him cool off a bit," he said to the other mechanics. "Give him a pit board and bring him in next lap!"

Manning ignored the signal.

Twice he raced past the board. Maybe he didn't see it. Maybe he didn't want to see it. Maybe it was his way of saying, 'I've cocked things up with these houses but I am still a winner.' Four laps later, Manning returned the Mustang to the pit area. The mechanics dropped into a well-rehearsed drill. Check the tyres, check all the engine fluids, get the car ready to go out on track again ASAP.

Fryer was having none of it.

"What's the point of showing you a pit board if you ignore it?"

"Yeah, sorry Howard. I got a bit carried away."

"That's not the bloody point. If the board says come in, you come in. I know you're the boss, but I look after the car.

We agreed you were going to check it out, not try and set a new lap record."

"Fair comment, Howard, but the car is awesome. You and the boys have done a brilliant job. As soon as it's ready, I'll go out again and finish testing."

"Okay, but we should both remember that we rely on each other. Now go and put a few more laps in before we wrap things up for the day."

Once again, Victor Manning had managed to talk himself out of a hole, and once again, it was a hole he had dug for himself.

Ray Stone sat in the waiting room while the medics carried out their examinations on his workmen. The minutes turned into an hour. An hour is a long time when you are alone with your thoughts and fears. Had he inadvertently exposed his men, his mates, to danger? And what sort of danger? His mind flashed back to the newspaper reports of the coroner's inquiry and the comments made. He was aware that accusations had been made against Manning and that Andy's comments had influenced the coroner, but that was all he knew. He was beginning to wish he had read the articles with more interest. His thoughts at the time were that some nosey parker had stuck his beak into his boss's business and temporarily put him out of work. Now he was beginning to change his mind. What if his boss was risking more than saving a few nails or skipping the odd timber joist?

Eventually a doctor emerged from the emergency cubicle.

"To be honest, we don't know exactly what we are dealing with here. It's some sort of threat to the respiratory system. We have managed to stabilise it but I'm not at all sure about the long term situation. It is possible that there will be some damage to the lungs that may be irreversible."

"Yes or no doctor, could they die?"

"Yes."

Ray left the hospital and drove home slowly. He switched on the car radio, hoping that the cacophony of sounds would take his mind off his workmen. But it did not help. The sight and sound of them gasping for breath would not leave him.

It didn't take the residents of the surrounding houses long to realise that the remedial work on the condemned properties in Hollybush Close had stopped. Builders are obvious, they always park their vans anywhere they can and usually there is a radio playing away to itself. One day of peace and quiet is enough to know that something has changed, and the observant amongst them would have seen the arrival of the ambulance and the paramedics. Putting two and two together and coming to the right answer would never have been easier.

Ray was in no mood to settle when he arrived home. He had called the families of his workmen from the hospital and he knew that they would be demanding answers from him. Why would fit, healthy, strong men be reduced to gasping, breathless wrecks just doing their job as builders? And what if they died? How many more deaths would be laid on Victor Manning's doorstep?

TWENTY-THREE

Andy and Susan were settling down to enjoy their evening meal. They had picked up a bottle of wine from the shop on the way home and were anticipating a quiet night in together. But their peace was broken by the ringing of the telephone.

"Andy? Look, sorry to bother you, mate, but have you heard about the latest tragedy at Hollybush Close?"

"Who's this calling?"

"Sorry, it's me, Jack from the newspaper. I thought you might want to know that two of Manning's workers have been admitted to the hospital and at the moment, between you and me, it doesn't look too good for them."

"No, I haven't heard. Frankly, there is no reason why I should. What actually happened?"

"They were working on the contaminated houses and appear to have been attacked by the same respiratory virus that killed the Jones baby."

"Well, there's no love lost between me and Manning's workers, but I certainly don't wish this on them. Thanks for letting me know, Jack. I suppose there is a good story in it for you, but I've had enough of Manning and his dodgy dealings. I'm trying to put it all behind me and get on with my life."

"Well, good luck with that. Frankly, I don't think that's going to happen because you are stuck right in the middle of it. I can only see you getting in deeper and deeper. If I hear any more, I'll let you know."

"Yeah, thanks for that, cheers for now."

No sooner had Andy finished the call when the phone rang again.

"Look, I'm sorry to bother you, mate, but I think we need to talk."

"Who is this, and what do we need to talk about?"

"My name is Ray Stone. I am Victor Manning's site foreman, or I was until earlier today when I walked out. I think we had better talk as I have two workmen in the hospital, who, as we speak, are fighting for their lives."

"Yeah, go on."

"We were working on cleaning up those houses, you know the ones. They've caught some bug or other and at the moment it doesn't look too good for them."

"Frankly, I've had enough of dodgy houses and builders who blame me for their boss's actions. I'm not sure I want to get any more involved. Anyhow, I don't see how I can help you. I think what happens is between Manning and the authorities."

"That's not quite true, is it? I heard you were some sort of campaigning vigilante, standing up for the tenants who had been given a rough deal."

"Yeah, a rough deal by your old boss, the housing association, and I suppose the council. In fact, it's difficult for some of these folks to get a good deal anywhere. But that doesn't make me Mother Teresa. I'm just a normal bloke trying to make a quiet living for myself but I hate to see someone rich like your old boss taking the mickey out of people who can't help themselves. Look, we're going round in circles. If you want, we could meet up, but I'm not sure what it will achieve."

"It would make me feel better if I could talk to you and maybe tell you what I know about Manning and his operation. I know in the past you've had a run in with some of the men but I really think we should work together to make sure Manning gets what he deserves."

With that they rang off, having agreed to meet at a local pub the following day.

When Andy related the two telephone conversations to Susan, at first she was concerned that Ray Stone was out to get Andy, some sort of revenge for being laid off work and eventually losing his job. In his own mind, Andy was fairly confident that the phone call was genuine and that Ray really wanted to make amends and get to the bottom of things. As best they could, they settled down to enjoy the rest of their evening.

Later that evening, in bed, they shared a brief goodnight cuddle. For once Andy felt he had let Susan down. Her movements, her sighs, suggested she wanted more but he couldn't forget the phone calls and what he might reluctantly, very reluctantly, be getting himself into.

Sleep did not come too easily.

Andy was deep in thought when Ray Stone walked into the bar. This stuff with Manning was playing on his mind, but he had other issues that were troubling him. Afterall he and

Susan were trying to run a business. Whilst neither of them were under any direct pressure, they were both very aware that for their partnership, both business and personal, to survive, it needed total commitment from both sides. More importantly, was Susan aware of the shady deals Manning and her husband had been cooking up over the years?

His private thoughts were interrupted as Stone introduced himself.

"Andy? I'm Ray Stone. I recognised you from the coroner's court. You probably didn't see me I was in the public gallery but I remember you. If you don't mind me saying, for a bloke who sells antiques you get around a bit."

"Yeah, well, I guess it's a case of being in the right place at the right time, except I think I was in the wrong place at the wrong time! Look, Ray, I realise that I am already involved and frankly, I feel proud to have brought all this out into the open, but, I don't see where we go from here and I'm not sure I want to go anywhere with it."

"Andy, I get that, but look at it from my point of view. I've worked for Manning for fifteen years and I've seen at close hand some of his tricks. Spacing out joists and nails is one thing, most firms do it but building on contaminated land is different. Having the local planning inspector in your pocket and getting him to grant building permission for unsafe sites is something else. Worse than that, selling these substandard houses to a housing association, who in turn will rent them out to struggling families, is well out of order. He always makes sure that the upmarket houses are finished to a high degree, you know, the ones that are sold for proper money but the others he could not care less about. And all the time his picture is in the newspapers, either opening another prestige development or winning another bloody motor race."

"Hang on, Ray. Are you saying that the planning officer is definitely in cahoots with him?"

"No doubt, they are as thick as thieves. It's been going on years."

"So where do I fit in Ray? If you know the history, talk to the newspapers, tell them what you've told me. What do you need me for?"

"Look, I'm a builder. I'm okay on a building site talking to the lads or here in a pub talking to you, but talking to those posh people, journalists, lawyers and the like they'd have me tongue tied in minutes. I would be like a rabbit caught in car headlights. No, it's down to you. You have the gift of the gab. I've heard you and you don't take any nonsense. I'll tell you what I know, which is plenty, but you have to let everyone else know what he's been doing."

Ray carried on talking. To Andy, it felt like he was listening to a confessional, all that was missing was 'Father, I have sinned'. There were waterlogged sites that needed to be drained, but of course they weren't. There were uneven sites that required levelling, again, this wasn't done, resulting in mud slides and ultimately damp conditions in the properties. The list went on, insulation missed out, houses passed on to housing associations with plaster that hadn't been allowed to dry properly. The list was almost endless.

Rather like a criminal who confesses his crimes to reduce his sentence, Andy knew that Ray wanted to clear his conscience and perhaps passing the knowledge of what he had been a party to, onto someone else somehow lessened his burden.

"Okay, Ray! Look, if I dig deeper into this and if I find anything that I can pass on to the newspapers, will you back me up? I do not want to be left high and dry."

"Too right I will."

With that they left after agreeing to keep in touch. Andy walked quickly back to the shop. As he walked, his mind was working in overdrive. There were so many questions that needed answers, and many of the answers might involve Susan, or, more accurately, her husband. The most important question that he asked himself over and over again was, *Am I prepared to risk everything that Susan and I have together just to bring an unscrupulous, ruthless builder to account?* Would Susan stand by him while he dragged her friend Victor Manning, and in all probability her husband, through the mud? Did the satisfaction he would get from nailing the two of them outweigh the hurt and pain it might cause Susan? Would his new, wonderful, amazing Susan see things differently?

TWENTY-FOUR

Susan talked endlessly through their evening meal. She was excited. It had been a good day at the shop. While Andy had his meeting with Ray Stone, she had been busy. One customer had bought an early nineteenth-century coffee table, another a silver tea service, plus there had been a few low value sales, bits and pieces of jewellery. In all it had been an interesting and profitable day.

By the time they finished eating, Susan realised she had been talking to herself.

"Is everything alright, Andy? I've been talking away and suddenly I've realised you haven't answered me. In fact, you've hardly said a word since you came back from seeing that builder guy."

"Sorry Su, I've got a lot on my mind, all of it concerning that bloody Victor Manning. Look, can we talk? I mean *really* talk."

"Of course. Sorry, I've been going on about the shop, it didn't occur to me to ask about your meeting. I'm sorry."

"Yeah, I'm sorry too baby, but that builder guy was Manning's chief foreman, and it seems that he has been building dodgy houses for years. Apparently, the big houses on his estates are built to a better standard than the smaller ones. By a better standard, I mean the smaller houses, those destined to be rented out, are barely habitable, whilst the big expensive ones have all the whistles and knobs. He quoted a whole catalogue of shortcuts and very dubious practices. As I see it, there are two issues here. Do I really want to get involved? And if I do dig deeper and find that your husband is in some way involved."

She interrupted him before he had finished speaking. "Look, I've already told you once, in fact, if I remember right, I've told you at least twice, that my life with my husband is over. It has been over since that day I brought round that old table for you to restore. You give me so much more than he ever did. Andy, we have a life together, a real life. I never had that before. With my husband, I lived in his shadow and of course, we both lived in Victor Manning's shadow. I cannot live thinking about yesterday. I need to look forward to tomorrow. And I so want to share that with you. For goodness' sake, Andrew Packford, I love you! Look! Do whatever you think you have to, just promise me that you'll take care. Please, just mind how you go. That's all I ask."

There it was again. 'Mind how you go,' That was the third time he had heard it.

Susan leaned across the dining table and kissed him gently on his forehead.

"We don't need to get up early tomorrow. We can leave the washing up. Let's have an early night."

For once Andy did exactly as he was told.

Angela buzzed the phone in Manning's office.

"Mr Manning, there is someone on the line who insists on talking to you, but he won't give his name."

"I don't need to talk to someone I don't know."

"I really think you should. He's making my life a bit uncomfortable on the phone."

"Okay, put him through."

"Mr Manning? Before you put the phone down, just listen to what I have to say. My name is Andrew Packford. I didn't tell your secretary because I knew you wouldn't have taken the call."

"You're bloody right, you interfering nuisance. I've only got two words to say to you. In case you don't know what they are."

Andy cut him short. "I didn't phone you up so that we could swear at one another. I phoned to offer you a deal."

"I get it. You want a pay-off. Why does that not surprise me? You know what you can do, sunshine!"

Andy interrupted again. "Yeah, but I don't need the deal, you do. Here's how I see it. I can offer you the chance to keep your millions, keep your workforce working and look like a hero."

"I've got my own plans in that direction. I don't need you or anyone else to tell me how to run my business."

"I thought you might say something like that. The way I see it, Mr Manning, all your previous deals have been, to say the least, dubious and possibly crooked. I'm not sure you would know an honestly built house if you saw one. Don't you think you owe some of your past customers some sort of recompense? You really could come out of this a hero or I could go to the newspapers with the full story of botched construction and unsuitable sites. Not to mention the collusion of the council's own planning officer."

"I don't know what your game is, but hell will freeze over before I will give you any money."

Before Andy could tell Manning that he didn't want his money, the line went dead.

After several minutes thought, Manning picked the phone up again and called Mark Seymour into his office.

"How are things going on the foundry site? How far advanced are the plans to get it de-contaminated?"

"As you know, Mr Manning, it is a large site. They have surveyed and cleared some of it. That area is now completely clear of contamination. They are waiting to move into the other area that is most at risk. That will be the next phase. Their initial survey should start in a few days."

"Okay. We need to get a move on."

Seymour interrupted, "But Mr Manning, you said you wanted a proper job. No shortcuts. That all takes time. The firm I'm using is one of the best in the business. They are not fast but they are thorough, I thought that was what you wanted."

"Yeah. But suddenly things have changed; we need to get moving. How many houses could we build on the area of the site they have already inspected? I'm suggesting we build where we can and turn the other areas into a community garden or wooded area; let the rabbits have the contamination, there's too many of the bloody things anyway."

"Yes, if that's what you want it may be possible. We could probably build a hundred houses on the already cleared area, possibly more."

"Okay. Set things in motion, draw up the plans. Let's go for one hundred houses in total, fifty percent our usual mix of three four and five bed houses for the punters, and fifty percent two or three bed terraced for the rental market. Don't forget to emphasise the community garden. Draw lots of trees on the plans, they like that kind of thing. Look, we must get this second, revised application accepted. Make it sound good. Out of the goodness of our hearts, we are building more affordable houses, all that kind of thing. Don't mention contamination. If anyone remembers all the fuss from the first application, we'll just say this area is completely clear. Show the planning committee the report on the clear area if you must, but for Christ's sake, don't let the decontamination people anywhere near the hearing. Don't forget they work for us, not the bloody council. How long will it take to get the application up and running? I'm hoping we can get it submitted in time for the next meeting of the planning committee."

"Yeah, that should be possible, Mr Manning."

"Good job, Mark, go for it."

Seymour left Manning's office trying to remember the last time the boss had used his Christian name.

Manning made another phone call. He had to look up the number before dialling. It had been a long time since he last needed to use it. There were no pleasantries, no, 'how are you?' Just business.

For a couple of weeks, Andy and Susan enjoyed their time together. She worked in the shop every day, except Friday, auction day. Andy busied himself in his small workshop, repairing and restoring. Happy at work, happy together at home.

TWENTY-FIVE

Most days in the shop followed a similar pattern. She never rushed to open in the mornings. There was no point in opening on the dot of nine o'clock because most of her customers were not around until mid-morning. Maybe a supermarket or a garage might have customers waiting on the doorstep but not an antique shop, so she was slightly surprised to see a dirty old van parked outside as she approached. She thought it might be another dealer doing the rounds of smaller shops, looking for new stock. Although she kept her little van spick and span, she knew too well that most dealers drove around in old bangers that they had little thought about keeping clean.

She looked across at the van as she unlocked the shop. The two men did not look like normal antiques dealers. But hey, what does an antique dealer look like?

They followed her through the open door and closed it behind them. As she switched on the lights and readied herself for the day, they looked around the shop.

"Ere luv! 'Ow old is this teacup?

"Well actually it's part of a trio, that is a cup and saucer with a plate and it's very early nineteenth century. It is nice, isn't it? They would make a lovely present for someone special."

"Oh, careless me. Look, I've just dropped it. My old mum always said I was a butterfingers didn't she, eh Charlie?"

"You did that on purpose!" Susan exploded.

"In that case, the saucer and plate might as well match it. Do you know, a little bird told me that your fella does all the repairs? Is that right? In that case, he would be a long time repairing this lot. He probably wouldn't have any spare time for ages. For instance, he wouldn't have any time to poke his nose into someone else's business, would he? Do you get my drift?"

Susan realised this was some sort of message but at that moment she was rooted to the spot, too scared to respond, not totally sure what they were getting at. All she wanted was for this particular scene to end and for them to leave her alone.

"If your bloke was to get this fixed up quickly and go out and about and poke his nose in where it's not welcome, we might see you again, luv do you know what I mean?"

"Just get out! Just get out!

They laughed between themselves and casually strolled out of the door into the battered van. There they sat for a few minutes, glaring at the sight of Susan slowly clearing up the tiny pieces of broken china. She locked the door and waited for them to go.

They drove off slowly.

Susan held her breath as she saw the van turn around in the road and head back in her direction.

They slowed as they passed the shop. Susan was shaking and scared but determined that these two thugs would not see the distress that they had caused her. As they passed, she pretended to rearrange the window display and despite the fear she was feeling, she used every muscle in her body to keep her composure.

The two in the van kept up the pressure by smiling and winking at her as they passed.

Once she was sure they were out of sight, she fell apart. The financial loss was not that important; what scared her was that she didn't understand why they were there. Was it just a random act of vandalism by a couple of neanderthals? What did they mean about her bloke poking his nose in? Surely it wasn't a threat from another dealer or a disgruntled customer. She didn't even think they had any unhappy customers. When she was sure they had gone and the nightmare was over, she felt the tears well in her eyes. She had held herself together while they were there, she would not let a couple of lowlifes see her tears, but now, just a few minutes later, it was different. The tears flowed down her cheeks like a waterfall.

When she was sure that she could make the call without breaking down, she phoned Andy.

"I'm sorry to bother you, Andy, I know you're in the workshop, but I've just had a funny thing happen in the shop. No. I don't know why I said that because it wasn't funny at all. I've had a couple of really nasty men in here. Breaking things and making veiled threats that I don't really understand. The threats seemed to be aimed at you. I think they wanted to scare me and they did a good job of it. Andy, can you please come and pick me up. I can't stay in the shop on my own today."

"Oh, Su. Try not to worry, lock the door, stay out of sight and I'll be there in a few minutes. Any sign of them coming back before I get there, just phone the police."

Ten minutes later, Susan breathed a sigh of relief when she saw Andy's BMW pull up outside the shop.

She was quiet on the short drive back to the apartment. Once safely inside, she couldn't hold back her emotions. The tears flowed and her body shook.

Andy had never seen her like this. To him, she was a strong-willed yet gentle woman who knew her own mind. She lived in her own space, a space he considered himself lucky to share, but now she was inconsolable. She sobbed like a child.

Andy was with her, next to her, holding her. But he waited until he felt she was ready to tell him her story. In her own time, she told him of the scruffy old van and how she thought it unusual.

Andy was aware that the phone was ringing.

"Don't worry about the phone, Su, just carry on when you feel ready. If it's anything urgent they'll leave a message."

She told him the full story. The broken china. The threats about him going out, whatever that meant.

It took a long while for her to return to the old Susan. The Susan he realised he was head over heels in love with.

"Look, Su, for the next few days I'll work in the shop, you stay here and take things easy. We have got plenty of stock; I don't need to be in the workshop all the time. We can leave the shop closed for the rest of today. I'll go in tomorrow. Right now, I'll make us a cup of tea and later I'll pick up a takeaway for supper. Can you just check who that phone call was from? Do we want to talk to them or was it someone selling double glazing?"

Andy was in the small kitchen making the tea when Susan checked on the missed phone call.

"It was the guy from the local paper. His message said he wanted to tell you something that he thought might interest you."

"Oh yeah, did he say what?"

"No, he said he would phone back later."

They didn't discuss the incident in the shop anymore. Susan had obviously been badly shaken up. Andy didn't attach too much importance to it and he reasoned that the more they talked about it, the more Susan might blame herself, which of course was nonsense. If you are in business, you have to expect the occasional hiccup. Andy knew only too well that some people are not nice, but everyone has to share the same world. You just have to get on with it.

They didn't get many opportunities to spend their days together. Evenings and night times were theirs, but daytimes were generally spent working. So, they made the most of this unexpected day off. Andy did everything he could to take Su's mind off what had happened. They watched TV and laughed at the programmes that showed the improbable antics of would-be antique dealers and equally improbable valuations, followed by cookery programme after cookery programme. Until they couldn't take any more.

"I'll go and get that takeaway now. What do you fancy, Chinese or good old fish and chips?"

"I'll leave it to you."

"Right, Chinese it is. Back in a few minutes."

By the time Andy returned Susan had prepared the table and opened a bottle of wine.

"I think we are both ready for this." She said.

"I know I am." Andy replied.

They had just finished their meal when the phone rang again.

"I suppose I had better take this call." Andy said as he reached for the telephone.

"It might be your new best friend from the newspaper. He said he would call back. You never know, it might be an interesting piece of news." Susan joked.

"Yeah, and it might not."

Susan was right, it was the reporter.

"Look, Andy, I thought you might want to know, your mate Victor Manning has just submitted a new application to build on the old foundry site. If you believe the hype he included in his plans, he's turned into a tree hugger. Large areas of trees and green spaces for everyone to enjoy. You probably know the kind of thing. The plans will go before the planning committee on Friday next week."

"If he's planting trees instead of building houses there has to be a good reason why. Probably because there's a swamp there or something. Listen, I'm glad you called. One of his long-time foremen contacted me. Apparently his dodgy building has been going on for years and his man was prepared to spill the beans, I don't know if there is a story in it for you? To be honest, I'm fed up with the whole thing. At the moment I've got enough agro of my own."

"What agro have you got, Andy? Tell me. You know a problem shared is a problem halved and all that kind of thing."

"Well, since you asked, Susan had a couple of neanderthal yobs terrorising her in the shop today. Being threatening and breaking stuff. Making veiled threats about me getting out and about. Frankly, I haven't a clue what they meant."

"Andy! You need to mix with the real world. Manning has just announced his latest building development and you get threats about going out. Could they have said anything about you sticking your nose in? It sounds like some form of intimidation to me."

"Do you know, you could be right. I'm so wrapped up in other things that I never thought of that. Would he stoop that low?"

"Would he stoop that low? Andy, if this development goes ahead, he stands to make about thirty million gross. That must be at least five mil net after costs. And this is a man who would skin a turd for a pound."

"That's a nice turn of phrase, but I get the gist of it"

"Look, give me the details of what went on in the shop and we'll run it in our local news section, it might make him think twice about any more tricks. Obviously there won't be any name calling, we don't want to get sued, but he'll know alright."

"Yeah, okay Jack. I'll leave it to you. We might have to meet again if I am going to pass on what his foreman told me. I'll get in touch with you when things settle down a bit. I could do without it but I suppose I had better look into his latest plans and have my say at the planning meeting."

With that, Andy told the reporter about the incident in the shop and after agreeing to talk later, they finished their conversation.

On the short drive home to Telcote Manor, Manning's cell phone rang. There were no pleasantries, no 'hello' just a voice telling him it had been done.

Andy sat next to Susan on the sofa and gave her a reassuring cuddle. He knew that in the coming days he would need to make himself familiar with Manning's latest plans, but for now his priority was Susan and her wellbeing. Manning could wait. For now.

The events of the day had made a big impression on the two of them. Initially, he and Susan did not realise why their business had been targeted, it was only after the conversation with the news reporter and being told about Manning's latest development plans that the truth began to sink in.

Susan was still scared by what had happened. Andy was trying hard to hide his anger. He knew that nothing Manning or his hirelings could do would detract him from doing what he believed to be right. Whilst Susan was his main priority, he kept seeing flashes of the mothers he had seen in Hollybush Close and their overwhelming desire to protect their families. For the next week or so he would run the shop and if they came back, they would face him this time. And he would be ready.

The first week in the shop went smoothly for Andy. Yes, he was a little concerned every time a strange car or van parked outside, but as the days went by he settled down to the point where he didn't look any more.

He knew the planning committee would be discussing Manning's latest proposals on Friday, the day after tomorrow. He had read the documents on the internet and he reasoned that the proposed green areas of the site must hide something, but he didn't know what. Whatever the trees concealed, he would attend the meeting and follow the proceedings.

He was deep in thought and didn't hear the shop door open. He did hear it slam shut. The sudden noise got his full attention.

"Oh look! We've got the main man this time. Now that's lucky, innit."

Andy looked straight ahead. Not left or right or up or down, just straight ahead. There were two men. He didn't know if they were the same two who had threatened Su, but he reasoned they probably were.

They were both heavy-set, although the one on the left was slightly smaller. Both were dirty and scruffy. Andy thought, *'If these two are Manning's hired muscle, judging by their appearance, he doesn't pay them very much. Maybe there was an intermediary who creamed off the lion's share of the money.'*

"Hi fellas, something I can do for you?"

"As it happens, there is. You can stay at home with that lovely missus of yours for the next few days."

"Why should I do that?

"Well, I think she would enjoy the company. To be honest, I wouldn't mind spending a bit of time with her myself. The other thing is, you're not popular in certain places, if you get my drift."

The prospect of what might follow didn't faze Andy too much, but he knew that timing was everything. He decided to play the scared shopkeeper and wait for the right moment.

"Now fellas, this is how I see it. I don't want any trouble and I would appreciate it if you didn't break any more of my stock. You have made your point, now will you please go. If you don't, I will be forced to call the police."

The prospect of him calling the police had the effect he was expecting, they started laughing and mocking him. "No, not the police! Oh, we are scared now. Yeah, we're crapping ourselves, aren't we?"

Andy played along. He was waiting for the right moment. He knew it would present itself, it was just a matter of timing.

"I'm not joking! I will call the police!"

At that point, the larger man on the right, swept his hand over an adjacent display table, knocking china and glass vases to the ground.

Andy responded, being careful to keep in character as the petrified antique dealer. "Look what you've done! Some of this stock is very old and valuable. You'll have to pay for that!" As he spoke, he moved closer, feigning to pick up the fallen bits and pieces.

Things were moving quickly now.

As the two hoodlums laughed and joked with each other, Andy knew this was the right time.

He was bent over the broken items. The nearest thug was now slightly ahead of him and half a meter to his left. Andy straightened his body with a corkscrew action, spinning to his left. The momentum turned his right fist into a lethal weapon as it made contact with the big man's ear. The sudden unexpected force rocked him on his feet. He tried to steady himself with his arms, which left his face vulnerable. No sooner had Andy's right fist made contact with his ear than his open left palm crashed into the thug's nose. Blood was everywhere. His nose was broken. Blood and mucus covered his face. Blood trickled from his ear. A split second was all it took.

The smaller man was now supporting his partner in crime, half carrying, half dragging him out of the small shop.

"Bloody hell! An easy fifty quid he said, the bastard. You are a bloody head case."

"No, you got it wrong. I'm just a normal bloke trying to lead a normal life. I don't need scum like you or Victor

Manning threatening me or taking advantage of other less fortunate people."

"Victor Manning? I don't know who you're talking about mate. The two of us might have had enough, but this ain't going away. He always gets the job done, one way or another."

The smaller man struggled to get his broken accomplice across the pavement and into the van.

Andy stood and glared. He was ready if it was some kind of ruse. It took a few seconds before the battered van started and eventually drove off. As before, they turned around in the road and drove back past the shop. But now they were in no position to glare threateningly into it.

Andy noticed the driver struggling with a mobile phone as he tried to support his semi-conscious accomplice and steer the old van all at the same time.

Satisfied that they had really gone, Andy returned his attention to clearing up the mess in the shop. He would wait until he was home before telling Susan of the day's events, and then he would only tell her what he thought she needed to know. No point in scaring the life out of her. As he finished tidying up, he sat and thought for a moment. The smaller man had said he didn't know Manning, Andy reasoned that he could be lying to protect his employer but he didn't seem bright enough. His first thought was that they looked like a couple of builders, particularly with the old van, but perhaps they weren't. Perhaps they were hired muscle, paid to keep his mind off Manning's next planning application.

Would Manning really go to those depths? Would he really hire what amounted to paid enforcers? How would he know where to go? Had he done this kind of thing before? Andy telephoned Jack at the local paper and told him about the latest episode. The newspaper had already run the story of the first visit the thugs had made to the shop. Jack promised to update the earlier article and run the story as some kind of vendetta against Andy and Susan. He finished the conversation by reminding Andy that Manning stood to clear five million pounds if this deal went ahead. Five million pounds! What would someone do for five million pounds?

It depends who you are. Some people might kill for a lot less than that.

"Think about it, I'm sure Manning would stop at nothing to get his hands on that sort of money. Particularly after the recent bad publicity."

"We all knew he was a ruthless bastard but this is in the realms of Hollywood fiction. Okay Jack, thanks for the heads up. I might need to take this a bit more seriously."

Andy spent the rest of the day planning his next move. Did he even have a next move?

He closed the shop a little earlier than normal and drove back to the apartment. In his usual way he shouted a greeting as he turned the key in the lock.

"Hi Su, I'm home!" Silence. "Are you there baby?" Silence.

He thought it strange that Susan hadn't replied. But he was home a bit earlier than expected, perhaps she had just gone out. It didn't take him long to check the small flat. It was obvious that Susan was not there. He wasn't too concerned, although she was normally there to greet him, she could have slipped out to the local shops. In fact, she could be anywhere. He wasn't at all bothered.

He made himself a cup of tea and settled in an easy chair to wait for her. The events of the day ran through his mind. The two heavies had obviously been told to frighten him away from the planning meeting but would Manning really hire someone to intimidate him? There was only one conclusion; it must be Manning. Who else cared about the meeting? But if the two did not know Manning they obviously weren't out of work builders with a grudge.

Whatever! He told himself that he wasn't worried, he could look after himself. He didn't want any trouble but he wasn't running away from it. Being his own man meant everything to him. He would go to the meeting, now more than ever.

Sitting comfortably, the time passed quickly. Susan still wasn't home. Now he was a little concerned. If she had planned to go out she would have left a note. He knew any message would have been left in an obvious place and he didn't see one. He looked in less obvious places, on shelves and bookcases, and he still didn't see one.

But he did find her purse and phone on a small shelf in the bedroom.

Now concern turned to worry. She was a modern lady. She would not go out without her purse or phone. He could not imagine why she would have left them behind.

He always thought of himself as being in control, never in a panic, not like the old days of driving the lorry when there was always a panic over something trivial. But now, today, his composure, his self-belief, was beginning to evaporate.

Victor Manning was behind this. Either directly or indirectly, he was responsible. He knew it.

Andy's world was beginning to fall apart. Should he leave the apartment and look for her? Where would he look? What if all this was in his mind and she had gone out for a perfectly rational reason? What if she should return while he was out? They could be chasing after each other for hours.

He knew he had to do something, he just didn't know what. Maybe he should take the bull by the horns and confront Manning, face to face. Even if Manning had played no part in Susan's disappearance, it would give Andy the chance to talk to him and present his own development proposal, the one that Manning had dismissed earlier without even hearing it.

Andy drove the few miles to Viman Development's office, deep in thought. He didn't know what he felt. He wasn't scared for himself, but he was concerned for Susan. If he was right in his thinking and the two thugs were sent by Manning, where would it all end?

He tried to tell himself that he was getting carried away. Yes, he would talk to Manning and if he got the chance, he would try to reason with him and suggest that he could build a new housing estate on a section of land that was adjacent to Telcote Manor. If he did that, he could build without the cost of buying land, as he already owned it. It would be a win-win deal for him. He would still make money, a lot of money. His men would be working and he would look like a hero to those who didn't know him.

The receptionist greeted him with a smile. "Hello, how can I help you?

"Hello, my name is Andrew Packford. I'd like to see Mr Manning, please."

"I'm sorry, sir, Mr Manning is out of the office for the next few days. Can anyone else help you?"

"No, it's Manning I need to see."

"He's actually on his way to Belgium. He's racing this weekend."

Somewhat deflated, Andy left the office and walked slowly to his car.

He knew Manning's staff would handle the planning meeting, there was no way the boss would attend and suffer humiliation should the plans get turned down. Also, if he wasn't there he could always blame his underlings for the failed proposal. If Manning was somehow behind Susan's disappearance, it would be very convenient to be out of the country. The bastard.

Andy was losing his confidence. What could he do? Who was he fighting?

His head was full of questions. He returned to his apartment. He needed to think.

The sound of the phone ringing interrupted his thoughts.

Susan!

"Hello, where are you, baby?"

"Ah, Mr Packford. How nice to talk to you? I'm sorry we can't meet in person but I understand from my employees that you are not an easy man to negotiate with. I had hoped that we could have avoided all the unpleasantness, but you seem to have other ideas."

"Who the hell are you?"

"Please don't interrupt. You don't need to know who I am but I'm in a position to help you reunite with the lovely Mrs Harrison."

"Listen, whoever you are. When I find you, and you had better believe I will, you will wish you had never heard of me. I assume the two dummies in the shop were your blokes? If that is the best you can do, you are dead, mate. Dead! Do you hear me?"

"Yes, very dramatic, I'm sure. You seem to have forgotten

that I can help you find your lady. Now, listen to me. Mr Manning is racing in Belgium this weekend at a place called Spa, I believe. I think it might be nice if you were to pop over to see him."

Where is Susan? Is she with him? The line went dead.

Andy tried to trace the caller's number but it had been withheld. He had no number, no address, no clues as to where he should go first. Dealing with a certain situation is one thing, but not knowing what you are dealing with is something else.

Now his head was spinning.

He needed to slow down, to take things one step at a time. What would happen if he didn't follow his instincts? What would happen if he went to the planning meeting and called their bluff? Surely, they wouldn't take personal revenge on Susan, would they? What sort of revenge?

He forced himself to slow down. His brain was going at ninety miles an hour but not actually moving forward. Sit. Quiet. Think.

It was now late afternoon on Wednesday; the meeting was on Friday. Manning would be in Belgium until late Sunday, possibly even Monday, and Spa racing circuit was about six or seven hours' drive away. Thinking about the logistics didn't help, but it did put things into perspective.

He could go to the police.

But what would he tell them? What would they do that he could not?

He had one complete day, twenty-four hours, to find her before Friday. If she was in England it might not be too difficult, but if Manning had taken her and she was in Belgium it could be a lot harder.

The whole scenario had now changed. Andy knew he

was going to stop Manning. He was going to get Susan back and someone, maybe everyone, was going to pay.

The only positive connection between him, Susan and the people behind her abduction was the shop. Maybe the thugs had dropped something, a note or piece of paper, or anything.

He drove back to the shop. There was nothing on the floor, just the remnants of the broken vases. He thought about exactly what had happened. They had come in and thrown their weight around, he in turn had retaliated and they had struggled out into the van and left.

No clues. Nothing.

As Andy was thinking, he was aware of a commotion outside the shop. Car horns were blaring and some motorist clearly wasn't very happy. He looked out of the window to see a car struggling to perform a three-point turn in the road. The same manoeuvre that the thugs had made earlier in their van. That was the piece of luck Andy was waiting for.

His shop had a security camera covering the door. It also covered the pavement area, and if he was lucky, it would cover the rear of a car or van doing a three-point turn.

He quickly ran through the recordings to find the scene of the two thugs coming in, followed by them leaving. As they attempted a three-point turn in the road the camera captured a clear image of the number plate. Bingo!

All he had to do now was find someone who could trace the van and give him the owner's name.

He remembered the reporter from the local newspaper. Maybe he had a contact in the police, someone who could check the computer and give him a name and an address. It was a slim chance but the only one he had. He made the call.

"Blimey, you don't want much, do you? I'm only a hack at the local paper not Interpol!"

"Yeah, I know, and it's cheeky of me to ask, but just now I'm struggling a bit. I just need something to give me an edge and this is all I've got. At the moment, Jack, you're all I've got."

"Okay, okay, spare me the sob story. I might know someone who can help. It will probably cost you a couple of bottles of single malt. I'll get back as soon as I can."

"Cheers, mate, I owe you one."

Twenty minutes later the phone rang.

"Right, you didn't get this from me, okay. But the van is registered to a so-called security firm; apparently they supply door minders, bouncers, that sort of thing. Andy, if this still has a connection to Manning, you need to seriously watch how you go."

"Jack, I'm grateful, mate, really grateful, but don't keep telling me to watch how I go. It's the others who need to watch out. Believe me, before this is over someone is going to wish they had never messed with me. Thanks again and I owe you one."

The address Jack gave him was only a couple of miles away. Andy knew it as a run-down part of town with mainly terraced houses that were in a bad state twenty years ago; now, they were waiting to be pulled down. In five years' time, there would be new modern houses in their place, but for now they were slums. Those that knew the area joked that the dogs went round in twos, one looking forward and one looking back, covering the rear.

Not wanting to draw attention to himself, Andy drove past the house at normal speed, just taking a quick glance

PETER COOMBS

to see the battered van parked at the kerb. The houses had small backyards that, years before, were just big enough for an outside toilet and a coal bunker. Nowadays the yards were filled with discarded bikes and rubbish. The houses in adjacent streets backed onto one another with just a small alley between, just big enough to allow residents to wheel the rubbish bins in and out.

He knew he was in the right place. None of the locals would care what went on under their noses, and in an area like this, there would be no problem recruiting not-too-bright hired help who were happy to flex their muscles for a few pounds.

He parked the BMW around the corner. He could see the house. It was the third house down the street. The van was parked outside, facing towards him. If anyone came out, he would see them. He waited twenty minutes, thirty minutes. Nothing. His mind was racing. He needed a plan At the moment, he had nothing but anger. He needed to know if Susan was in the house and who else was inside and if she wasn't there, where was she?

He checked inside the car, trying to think if there was anything that might help him. He couldn't find anything. No screwdriver, no tyre levers, nothing that might help. There was only normal stuff that people keep in their cars; maps, bits of paper, pens, old hats, basically junk.

He waited another twenty minutes. The sun had set some time ago and now it was quite dark. The few street lights that were working cast an eerie half glow over the derelict buildings. If he had a mind to think about it, the area actually looked better at night than during the hours of daylight.

Time was slipping away from him. He couldn't afford to wait any longer.

150

He left his car and walked past the end of the street into the alley between the yards. Third house down. It wasn't difficult to find the back of the house. There was a solitary light shining in a downstairs room. He walked through the hanging gate into the scruffy yard. There were no signs of life, no noise, just the single light. Andy approached the window slowly. Still no signs of life. If anyone was in the house, they were not in this room. He slid open the sash window enough to climb through but he didn't go in. He stayed hidden in the yard, crouching behind the rubbish bins. He searched around in the gloom and found an old tin which he threw against the house wall. Thirty seconds later a familiar face appeared at the open window.

A voice from deep inside the house called out. "What was that, Charlie?"

"I dunno. The window's open. I think it was kids mucking about, little sods. They should know better than to try it on here. If they are still there, I'll kick their arse."

The back door opened and the character Andy had last seen helping his accomplice out of his shop walked out. Still hidden behind the bins Andy watched and waited as the man walked through the yard into the alley. He stood and looked both ways, looking for the kids. He was still looking for kids as he turned to walk back through the broken gate. Andy sprung at him. A snapping, stamping action from Andy's right foot caught the side of his left knee.

He went down with a scream.

Andy dragged him back into the alley.

"I'm not here to muck about. You're already going to be limping for a long time, if you don't help me, you're going to be wishing you could limp. Where is she?"

"Where's who?"

"You know who. Susan, the lady in the shop."

"All I know is that the builder guy you are mixed up with wants to stop you appearing in some planning meeting. Honest, that's all I know. I don't know nothing about meetings, just that he doesn't want you there. For God's sake, man, this is nothing to do with me. I just get paid peanuts to do what he says. My mate's in there in a bad way after what you did to him earlier. We just do a bit of leaning for him, that's all, nothing heavy. But he can get nasty. I've heard them say there's a lot of money involved. This thing between you and that builder, I don't understand it, but I know it's big money. Honest, that's the truth."

"So where is she then?"

"She's not here. You can check if you want."

"Who's in the house?"

"Only me and my mate, and he's in a right state, thanks to you."

"Right, get back in the house. I'm going to be very close behind you so don't act any more stupid than you can help."

"How am I supposed to walk with this leg?

"That's your problem."

Slowly, they made their way through the small yard and in through the back door.

"Is that you, Charlie? Where have you been? What was all the noise for?"

"Yeah, it's me and I've got someone you've met before. It's that bloke from the shop."

The second thug was lying on a filthy bed, his face still covered in blood and gore, only now it was congealed and matted and disgusting.

"Look, give us a break, will you? We don't do the thinking, we're just his leg men. We just do what he says. God knows he doesn't pay us enough for the grief you're giving us."

"First things first. Who is your boss and where can I find him?

"Listen, you don't know who you're messing with. He's in the big league and he don't take prisoners."

"Last warning! I'm not here to make friends."

"You can say that again. Okay, okay, if I tell where he is, you didn't hear it from me, right? He likes to be called Jay but his real name is Jeremy Jaques. He gets right pissed off if someone calls him Jeremy. He lives in a big house a couple of miles away. If you know where the golf course is, he lives just past the entrance, on the right. You can't miss it. He always has his Porsche outside."

Andy knew where the golf club was and it didn't take long to find a big house with a Porsche outside. From the road, it looked like the sort of house that a successful businessman might own, or possibly an up-and-coming celebrity. Large and impressive but not particularly tasteful. In addition to the Porsche there was a nondescript people carrier, possibly a Volkswagen or a Ford, in the driveway.

The house looked quiet and, in a scary way, very ordinary. The neighbouring houses were similar and spaced out down the road with just enough gap between them to allow easy access around the property. He sat in his car just looking, not knowing what his next move might be. He didn't have to sit for too long. The front door opened, and a woman came out and got into the people carrier. He had to make a quick decision.

Was the woman involved in Susan's disappearance? Was Susan in the house and was she now unguarded? If the woman was involved, was Susan being held somewhere else?

The obvious answer was to follow the people carrier. At worst, it was a wasted journey, at best, it might lead him to Su. If all else failed, the woman might tell him where she was. If she had the information he needed, he knew that, eventually she would tell him.

He kept a few hundred yards behind the people carrier. After a mile or so, he knew where she was headed. He took a chance and overtook her, not looking as he drove past. He parked the BMW around the corner and waited. Presently she parked outside the third terraced house down the scruffy street. Before she had a chance to switch off the engine, he opened the passenger door and slid in.

"What the bloody hell are you doing? Who are you? Get out of my car!"

His right hand gripped her left arm just below the elbow.

"All my instincts tell me I should break your arm and in a few minutes I might, but I'm going to give you the chance to save yourself a lot of pain. Simple question; where is Susan?"

"I don't know any Susan. I've just come here to look after my brother. Some psycho gave him a right going over."

"That's the wrong answer. Your brother got what he deserved. He told me that Jay has Susan and I saw you leave Jay's house. So, I'll ask you again, where is Susan?"

"Look, my brother and his mate work for Jay, right. I work for him too. I look after his house clean it, cook his grub, that kind of thing but that's it. Honest. I don't know nothing about his business. This Susan woman is not at his house, I can tell you that. All I do know is that Jay has a lock up on an old industrial site. Maybe she's there. That's all I know. On my mother's life."

"Tell me where this lock up is and you can go and help your brother. I'm not interested in your lowlife family, you can do what you like to make a living, but if you're giving me the runaround, your brother will be needing a lot more help."

He sat in his car. He had memorised her directions to the lock up but before driving off he made a phone call.

Andy found the place, no problem. It was a large disused industrial site. Probably a thriving, working community years ago, now just a collection of old sheds and workshops. Some of them were still being used by chancers doing up the odd car. Discarded car bits were here and there. He parked on the approach road, well away from buildings, and waited.

Fifteen minutes later, he heard the rumble of a lorry. The air brakes hissed as it stopped next to his BMW.

"I know this is a big ask but I didn't know who else to turn to."

Harry Thornton grinned back, roll-up cigarette hanging precariously between his lips.

"I've got my phone here, just give me a bell when you're ready."

Andy left his car and set off on foot. He checked the various sheds and buildings, listening for any noise, any clue. As he went, he checked the various parked cars that littered the site. One hand on the bonnet was all he needed to know if the vehicle had been used recently. Most of the buildings had no doors and those that were being used by car repairers were locked from the outside. Eventually he found what he was looking for, a ramshackle building with two warm, late model cars outside and no padlock on the door.

He whispered into his phone.

"I hope you're right, mate." Harry answered. "Here goes my no-claims bonus."

Seconds later the tipper lorry came round the corner, gathering speed as it got nearer.

Without slowing, the giant truck ploughed through the two cars, pushing them yards across the gravel road. Broken bits of metal and plastic flew in all directions, shards of glass everywhere.

Two cars, two men, no problem. The first man through the door saw the rising cloud of dust covering what a few seconds earlier had been an expensive car. What he didn't see was Andy's leg across the doorway, nor did he see the crashing right hook that landed squarely on his left temple.

One down.

Man number two followed closely behind. Too closely. He couldn't stop himself tumbling over his accomplice. He was down but not for long. He quickly grasped what was happening and rolled to his right, narrowly avoiding Andy's kick. That mid-air kick had unbalanced Andy, who was now struggling to remain upright. Man two was up and on his feet. He wasn't interested in the wreckage, he knew he was fighting for his life. Andy was big and strong and the equal to most men, but he was an antiques dealer not a regular street brawler. For once he was out of his depth and in serious trouble.

Between the two men lay the comatose body of the first man. Whoever was going to make the first move would have to step over or around him.

The best battle plan is to make your enemy come to you and the further they come, the better. More time for you to think and more chance of them getting tired. So, Andy took a step backwards, making a bigger gap between them.

Man two took the bait and jumped over his stretched-out partner but fresh air between his legs didn't make for a firm footing. Andy threw the palm of his hand up and under the man's nose. As he landed his hands instinctively went up to his face. Game over.

Andy landed two, three crashing blows to his face and body. There would have been more but for Harry's intervention.

"For God's sake, Andy, we don't want to kill anyone, we just want to get Su back."

"Yeah. Thanks, mate. It's not easy keeping a lid on it when you know they're holding your lady. I swear, Harry, if they've hurt her or, you know, I'll kill all of them and Manning as well."

They were speaking as they were running into the building. The perimeter of the large shed was dark but the centre was brightly lit by a string of bare light bulbs fixed to a single cable. In the gloom around the edge were packing crates, some open and some nailed shut. Here and there were scattered workman's tools, hammers, screwdrivers, saws.

In the centre were two chairs and an old metal bed frame.

There was no trace of Susan.

"Oh shit! I hope I haven't made the biggest mistake of my life. Harry, if I've got this wrong and dropped you right in it, I'm so sorry, mate. I'll do everything I can to make it up to you."

"We're not done here yet, Andy, I think you've got the right place, what with two chairs for the minders and a bed for Su..."

"Harry, don't go there. I swear, man, I'll kill the bastards if they've as much as touched her."

"Let's not think about that, Andy. We'll just pull this place apart and see if we can find her, or maybe find out what's been going on in here. It looks well fishy to me."

They started down one side. Mostly they were moving empty packing crates. The crates were all similar but not quite identical. Made from wooden slats nailed together to form a square box with a separate lid. All the crates had the same markings on them. Neither Andy nor Harry recognised the language, maybe it was from a far eastern country, maybe it was something else. For the moment they really were not interested.

In the furthest corner, they pushed two crates out of the way and found what they were looking for.

Susan was crouching behind the crates, arms tied and a filthy rag stuffed in her mouth. She was shaking uncontrollably, tears streaming down her swollen cheeks.

Andy lifted her in his arms and gently laid her on the ground next to him, quickly untying her arms and freeing the gag.

"Oh. Baby! What have they done to you?"

"Andy. Andy. When I heard the crash and they went to check, I just got off that awful bed and ran. They had loosened the ropes round my ankles and were getting ready for a bit of fun. I really thought that they had come for me when you moved those crates. Oh, Andy, you can't imagine what I thought."

"Shush! It's all over now, Su, mainly thanks to Harry and that truck of his. Come on, let's go home."

Harry was looking at the abandoned crates. In the bottom of one he found a few discarded small boxes, picking one up he saw it contained automobile parts. More precisely it contained BMW brake pads. Clearly labelled, no mistake.

"Andy, these crates were full of car bits. Look at this box, it says genuine BMW brake pads. Why would they be shipped in a crate that appears to have originated in the Far East? You don't think we've stumbled on a counterfeit parts racket, do you? Looking at all these crates, they must have been importing them in massive numbers. You're definitely involved with some dodgy blokes."

"Harry, save it for later. Let's get out while these two goons are still resting. If you're interested, grab a couple of boxes and we could get someone to check them out. Better still, leave them all here. I can't do any more tonight. I'll call trading standards in the morning. Hopefully by the time they get here the casualties will have crawled off somewhere."

Andy helped Susan through the door, Harry followed. The two men were still on the ground and just beginning to stir. Andy knew that they did not present a threat, they had no fight left in them. Harry walked back to his lorry, which looked none the worse for it's encounter with the cars, while Andy and Susan returned to his car. Once inside they knew that for the moment at least it was over.

Once safely in their apartment, Andy and Susan exchanged their stories. Once more he was amazed by her determination and inner strength. How could someone so lovely, so delicate be so strong?

After a long, hot bath Susan fell into a deep sleep, safe in the knowledge that Andy would not be leaving her side. Not now. Not ever.

She slept like a baby, curled up in a comforting bed. Andy sat in a chair next to her. He couldn't sleep; he had too many things going through his mind. The day had started when the two thugs had tried to smash up his shop and had quickly moved onto the terraced house, the big house and ultimately Susan's release from the warehouse. All that while Victor Manning, the person who had caused all this grief, was enjoying himself in Belgium.

Andy knew that soon, very soon, Manning would get his just deserts. He could not ruin people's lives and get away scot-free. Somehow, he would pay.

He didn't really sleep. As soon as their office opened he phoned trading standards. The officer he spoke to knew all about the scammed car parts. Apparently it was a sophisticated operation. Counterfeit parts were made in the Far East to match the original makers' components. The counterfeiters targeted high-value cars like BMW, Mercedes and the like, and concentrated their efforts on brake pads, which, the officer said, were very easy to copy. Outwardly they looked the same similar packaging, identical size etc but crucially, they were made from rubbish material. The first few applications of the brakes was okay but subsequent braking was non-existent, the pads simply fell apart. Several accidents had been reported and several claims had been made against garages who had been duped into buying the fake items. They estimated that the market was worth several million pounds a year.

Andy told them everything he knew about the warehouse, Jeremy Jaques, everything.

He also called his favourite reporter at the newspaper. "Jack, I've got a scoop for you, Call it pay back if you like. I figure I owe you that."

"Too right you do. How did you get on with that security firm I told you about?"

"Jack, that's the scoop. Apart from supplying heavies for a bit of intimidation, the real money comes from importing fake car parts as far as I can make out, thousands of them, high-end stuff. Apparently, their speciality is brake pads for Mercedes and BMW etc. According to trading standards, the business is worth several million a year. I managed to find their warehouse; I also found the top man. If you take a photographer with you, you will find the warehouse being raided as we speak. If you're quick, you might get a double scoop and be there when they arrest Jeremy Jaques."

"Blimey! You have been busy. It was only yesterday I gave you the info on them. What has been going on?"

"If I told you, you wouldn't believe me, but there will be an even bigger story in a few days' time. But for now, you'll have to wait. I have got a lot of things on my mind at the moment, particularly Manning's planning application on Friday. Trust me, Jack, you need to be there as well." Andy passed on the addresses and finished the conversation.

When Susan woke it was mid-morning.

Andy spoke to her in a calm, reassuring voice. "Su, after what you have been through you need to take things easy for a few days. I'm not going to open the shop. I'll put a notice in the window. I'm sure our customers won't mind. I'll say we are having a couple of days' holiday."

"Some holiday I've had."

"I know, but I promise it is nearly over now and I'm not planning on leaving you alone again, ever!"

"Andy, what does that mean? 'Nearly over.'"

"Su, this all started because I got involved in Victor Manning's dodgy houses, I'm quite happy to sort things out my way, but Manning was behind you being taken hostage by those thugs and in my book that is way out of order. The plan was that it would keep me away from the planning meeting tomorrow. Well, that backfired on him and on his hired helpers. Now more than ever I'm determined to attend that meeting, and with the help of his old foreman I'm going to do my best to put him out of business. Unfortunately, it's going to look bad for your husband."

Susan interrupted him. "How many times do I have to tell you? I'm not interested in my husband. He is history. He will have to live with whatever the consequences are. He made the decision years ago to get involved with Manning and now he is stuck with it. Andy, it's *you* I care about and our future together. Please, please, promise me you won't get involved in anything that might destroy our future."

"I promise."

TWENTY-SIX

Several hundred miles away in the south west corner of Belgium, Victor Manning was showing his competitor's entrance pass to the half-asleep trackside security official. He casually waved him through the gates and into the busy race paddock.

It didn't take Manning long to find his race transporter and support team. Howard Fryer was waiting to welcome him.

"Did you have a good trip down here?"

"Yeah, fine thanks. I left the office on Wednesday and stayed the night in a nice little hotel just outside Brussels. How are things going here?"

"Yeah, we're okay. Arrived here early this morning. Me and the boys slept in the lorry overnight. We are good to go. The car's checked over, all good. Ready for the first practice session tomorrow."

"Listen, Howard, I'm booked into a small hotel a few miles away,I'm going to the race office to sign on, then I'm going to the hotel. I've got a few business issues to sort out. You and the boys can handle getting the car through scrutineering, can't you?"

"Yeah, sure."

With that, Manning strolled over to the office, stopping to talk to fellow competitors as he went.

Fryer turned to his mechanics.

"Well, the boss has buggered off to his posh hotel and left us to sort things for tomorrow, so we'll get down to scrutineering first thing in the morning and get the Mustang checked over. Usual rules, if there's anything not right, someone gets the sack. Now, let's all go and sample some Belgian beer."

He said it with a smile on his face. They all knew there was not the slightest chance of anything being wrong. Victor Manning's Ford Mustang was the best prepared car in the paddock.

In his hotel room, Manning called his office. His secretary had no messages for him except that someone had asked to see him personally and had left without leaving a message. Then he spoke with Mark Seymour.

"Is everything in place for tomorrow's planning meeting?

"Yes, Mr Manning. I've gone over all the small details with Mr Harrison. I'm sure we'll get the plans approved this time."

"We bloody better or we're all up shit creek. You make sure that Harrison tells the inspector that he completely endorses the scheme. I'm pretty sure we won't have any problems with that interfering antique dealer. I think he has othe, more pressing, things on his mind."

Seymour didn't understand what his boss meant but he was happy to agree.

Manning rang off and made another call. There was no answer.

He left his room and went downstairs to the bar. The barmaid had her back to him. When she turned around, she realised he had been looking at her, checking her over, checking the possibilities. In the five years she had worked at the hotel, she had poured drinks for and listened to the stories of countless racing drivers. Young, rich Italians might have made some impression on her, for them she would have smiled, but there were no smiles for this middle-aged Englishman with a wife at home. He would get his drink and no more.

Andy and Susan spent the rest of the day in their small apartment. He knew that she was still very fragile, the ordeal had taken a big toll on her. She was quiet and withdrawn. Andy tried to engage her in casual conversation but it wasn't easy. He didn't want to smother her but he didn't want to leave her to brood on her own. As the day wore on, he began to see the old Susan emerge. He didn't force things, he just let her take her own time. When he thought she was ready, he told her again about the planning meeting scheduled for the following morning.

"Look, after what I've been through, I want Manning and my conniving husband to get what they deserve. But and it is a big but I don't want you to get into any more trouble. No more fights. No more getting involved with lowlifes. Do what you have to do but remember, Andy Packford, I love you."

That was all Andy needed. He called Ray Stone and checked that he was prepared to speak at the meeting. Then he ran through in his mind what he would say himself. He was ready for Viman Developments.

On Friday morning Andy was not about to leave Susan alone, so they both met Stone at his house and the three of them drove to the council offices. It was obvious that Ray Stone was more comfortable working on a building site than talking to a council planning officer, but Andy explained the procedure and what might happen.

"Just explain things in a straightforward way, speak in your normal way preferably without the expletives. Remember, all these people are basically council workers. Just say what you know to be true. Unlike Manning and his underlings, do not make things up, just say it like it is."

They parked in the same car park that Andy had used a few weeks before when he and Harry Thornton had been accosted by Manning's disgruntled workers but now, as they walked to the council chambers, they saw Mark Seymour get out of his car and walk towards them.

"Hello Ray. What's this? Have you turned your back on Mr Manning and joined the opposition?"

"Yeah, you probably heard I walked out on him. Did he tell you why?"

Andy quickly interrupted him. "Not now, Ray, save it for later. Try and keep calm. There will be plenty of time to settle old scores when this meeting is over."

Seymour walked alone into the council chambers, followed by Andy, Susan and Ray Stone. Inside they took their seats, Andy and the others in the public area whilst Seymour sat next to one of his office colleagues and to Susan's shock, her husband Derek Harrison, the council's chief planning officer. As Seymour chatted to his colleague and checked over the details of their application, Harrison looked straight ahead. If he had seen his wife walk in with her new younger lover, he showed no indication that it bothered him.

The chairman called the meeting to order and outlined the proposed application to the planning committee. "As the committee may remember, Viman Developments submitted an earlier proposal to develop this site, and after due consideration it was decided to postpone our decision until such a time that the applicant could provide proof that the area involved was clear of any contamination. Mr Seymour, for the benefit of the committee, can you please outline what measures Viman Developments have taken to ensure that your latest application is in accordance with government health and safety guidelines?"

Mark Seymour rose uneasily to his feet, tightly holding a sheaf of papers.

"Mr Chairman, members of the planning committee, I would like to apologise to all of you for presenting our previous application. At that time, everyone at Viman Developments realised the pressing need for new affordable housing and in our haste to deliver new homes we overlooked our responsibility to thoroughly check the site. Which, I would like to add, was the only site available to us at that time. With hindsight, we now realise that we should have investigated the sub-soil on that particular site more carefully. On behalf of Viman Developments, I am now happy to resubmit our proposals for this proposed development.

"You will see from the paperwork in front of you that we have had the site thoroughly tested and cleared where necessary by one of the leading specialist contractors in that particular field. May I also draw your attention to the large areas of green space that we have allocated for the estate. As you will see, this application is completely endorsed and supported by Mr Derek Harrison, the council's own chief planning officer. In conclusion, I would most strongly ask that the planning committee give these new plans their utmost and favourable attention. Thank you!"

"Thank you, Mr Seymour, I think you have made the position of Viman Developments very clear. This planning committee realises the desperate need for new affordable housing, something that is lacking in this area. We also appreciate the fact that these proposals have the full backing of Mr Harrison. Before I ask the committee to consider their decision, I would like to ask any members of the public present for any objections they may have."

Susan flicked her eyes across to Andy, As she did so, he rose slowly to his feet.

"Mr Chairman, I have looked at the plans and the proposed positioning of the houses. As Mr Seymour has told us, there are quite large areas of green space, more than might normally be expected. Whilst this would be to the benefit of the residents, I have to question why more homes are not planned to be built on these areas. To save us all reading pages and pages of very technical soil analysis, can Mr Seymour direct us to the page in the report that says the soil in these particular areas is suitable to be included in the scheme? While Mr Seymour is looking for those particular pages, may I make a few observations regarding the suitability of Viman Developments to carry out this work, or indeed any future building work?"

"Mr Packford, this is not the time nor place to make such scandalous comments."

"Mr Chairman, if the integrity of the developer cannot be questioned during the planning application, then when can it be questioned? We are all aware of the unfortunate deaths that were attributed to houses built by this company on a different estate. The same houses were being rectified by Viman's foreman, who is sitting next to me, until, that is, his workmen were overcome by toxic fumes. As we sit here arguing over Viman's suitability to build houses, one of his men is fighting for his life in hospital. Mr Ray Stone was Viman's senior foreman over a number of years and he is happy to tell this hearing that Manning systematically and regularly cut corners to save money and speed up the work. Shortcuts that, although small to begin with, escalated and ultimately resulted in the deaths of these unfortunate residents. Mr Stone is also prepared to swear on oath that Victor Manning himself ordered these shortcuts, which were overlooked by Mr Harrison and, under his instructions the entire team of building inspectors. Further events have recently happened to me and my partner, who was kidnapped in an attempt to stop me addressing this hearing. I am convinced that Victor Manning was behind these actions. The police are currently investigating my claims and I am sure that in due course you will be able to read about them in the press.

"Now, has Mr Seymour found the relevant pages, or should we forget that for the time being?"

No one spoke. No one. There was total silence.

Slowly, one by one, people began to talk in whispers. To begin with, they talked to the person sitting next to them, then they shouted to anyone and everyone. Seymour, Harrison the chairman, the committee. No one knew what to say, what to do. The flashguns from a dozen cameras lit up the room.

Susan turned to Andy. "Well, it beats going to the auction. Fridays will never be the same again. Andrew Packford, am I ever proud of you? You ask me about my husband well, I'll tell you, you may be a penniless antiques dealer but you are a giant of a man compared to him. May I live to be a hundred, I'll never forget what you did today."

"Order! Please, order!"

The chairman tried his best to restore some calm to the proceedings but the members of the public and the journalists wouldn't let him. People were leaving their seats to shake Andy's hand and slap him on the back. It was obvious to everyone that the meeting was over.

Seymour collected his papers and shuffled them into some sort of order. He looked over to where Andy and Susan were sitting and, after thinking about it, slowly walked over.

"Look, I know we're on different sides but I'm only doing my job, honest! Manning pays my wages and they feed my wife and kids. If I didn't do what he tells me, there would be a hundred others who would."

"Yeah, fair enough. I don't have any quarrel with you. I don't suppose sending a couple of losers to frighten me and having my partner kidnapped was your idea. But that is what your boss has tried and as you can see, it's backfired. I don't think you and I are ever going to be best friends, but you haven't done me any harm."

"Andrew can I call you Andrew?"

"Andy is better only my mother calls me Andrew."

"Well, Andy, I don't know what has happened between you and Manning and believe me, I know nothing about any kidnapping or heavies sent to scare you. All I do is design housing estates; that is what he pays me for. Over the years, I've known that he can get nasty if he doesn't get his way, but I never thought he would get involved with anything outside the law. Andy, between us, I think this is going to cripple Manning. We don't have any alternative sites to build on and as you guessed, this one is riddled with contamination, even after some of it has been cleaned. And the housing association is suing him for the loss of those toxic houses, so frankly, I think he is finished. Although it's probably not going to bother him too much; I think he's got millions stashed away."

"Yeah, I'm sure he has. As we're being honest with each other, I'm done with him now. For me, this is the end. All I know about his hired muscle, I've passed onto the police, they can deal with it. You might not think it, but all I want is a quiet life."

Somewhat begrudgingly they shook hands and went their own way.

While all the commotion was going on, Ray Stone had stayed very quiet. He was out of his depth in the meeting but he was no fool and, like Mark Seymour, he knew that Manning was ruined.

Andy, Susan and Ray slipped away quietly. They drove back to Ray's house in silence.

"I wish you luck, Ray. I suppose you will be looking for a new job now."

"Yeah, I guess so, I might consider a change of career. You never know, I could become an antiques dealer like you. But, judging by your experiences, it might be a bit too rough for me."

The three of them laughed. But there was nothing funny, nothing to laugh at. Ray Stone was out of work and, thanks to Victor Manning, he now had a dodgy reputation. Susan had broken any ties that might have remained between her and her husband. And Andy knew that this was only the beginning of the end. There would be police statements, court appearances as a witness and who knows what else. But for now, he and Susan were safe and together.

TWENTY-SEVEN

Early Friday morning, four hundred and thirty miles away in Spa, Belgium, the race circuit was manic, as they always are. Most of the race teams had arrived the previous day, having driven from all four corners of Europe. Heavy-eyed mechanics were emerging from their beds. For some, that might have been in a luxurious motorhome, for those less fortunate, it was a makeshift bed in the back of a lorry. Either way, they were all facing a busy weekend. The first task was to unload the race cars from the transporter, give them a check over and present the cars and drivers' clothing for scrutineering. The scrutineers check every aspect of the vehicle, primarily to ensure that it is safe in every respect, both for the driver and the other competitors. Next, they check that it complies with the various rules relating to the particular class the driver is competing in. Finally, they inspect the drivers' racing overalls to make sure they also meet the safety standards.

For all the teams it is a tense time. It's not unheard of for the scrutineers to have a difference of opinion with the team owner or his mechanics. But for Manning's car, meticulously prepared by Howard Fryer and his team, there were no such problems.

With the all-important sticker, that indicated the car was good to race, attached to the windscreen, the team settled down to wait for the driver.

"There's nothing more we can do 'til the boss gets here. He's probably still tucked up in some fancy hotel bed somewhere. You fellows go and get a coffee and chill for a bit, I'll stay here. When he turns up, I'll get you on your mobile."

With that, the mechanics walked off to the circuit restaurant and Howard settled down to wait for Manning.

At fifteen minutes past eight a.m. Victor Manning sat down in the small restaurant to enjoy his breakfast. After breakfast, he made a phone call. No answer. He thought it strange. That was the second time his call had gone unanswered.

Next, he called Howard Fryer.

"How are things there? Scrutineering okay?"

"Yes boss, no problems here. Practice starts after lunch. I take it you'll want to get as much in as possible."

"Yeah, I've got a couple of calls to make so I'll be with you in an hour or so. That should still give me plenty of time to practice."

Then he called his secretary.

"I'm sorry Mr Manning I haven't heard from Mark Seymour yet. He left the office early but the meeting wasn't scheduled to start until ten o'clock. I'm sure he'll call as soon as the planning committee makes their decision."

"Right. I'm still in the hotel at the moment, I'm leaving for the circuit now. Call me on the mobile as soon as you hear from him. We need to get this new site up and running quick smart. In the meantime, let the ground workers know that they can start on the site preparations tomorrow. We can't afford to waste any more time. We've got a lot riding on this."

"Yes, Mr Manning, as soon as Mark gives us the go ahead from the planning people I'll get things underway. We all wish you a safe and successful race."

He rang off and left the hotel.

As he walked to his Jaguar, the barmaid from last night was walking across the car park, ready to start another shift. He tried to engage her in conversation, but she ignored him. If he had bothered to turn around, he would have seen her giving him the finger.

A short drive later he was in the race paddock and talking to his mechanic. Fryer was explaining the changes they had made to the car since the Silverstone test a couple of weeks ago.

"We've changed the engine settings and managed to get a bit more power out of the motor."

The ringtone of Manning's mobile phone stopped the briefing.

"Sorry, Howard, I have to take this."

"What! You are kidding me! For God's sake, what's happening? Seymour, what do I pay you for? You and that useless prat Harrison. It's no wonder his bloody wife's left him. Can we salvage anything from this?"

"Mr Manning, you are not listening. The planning committee threw out our plans. This antiques dealer guy, actually, his name is Andy has claimed that Viman has been cutting corners for years and that Harrison has turned a blind eye. The police have arrested someone called Jeremy Jaques, who they say, on your instructions, threatened the antiques dealer and kidnapped his girlfriend. The media are all over this. It looks like Derek Harrison will get the chop, and several of his building inspectors with him. Mr Manning, we are in big, big trouble."

"Seymour, I thought you had this all sewn up. Can't I trust you to do anything? Do I have to do every bloody thing myself? I'll get on to Harrison and see if there's a way out of this mess."

"Mr Manning" Seymour interrupted. "This has all kicked off in the last half hour or so and it's already overwhelming; the press are everywhere, Mr Harrison hasn't returned to his office and we have received emails from the housing association to the effect that they are going to sue the company over the contaminated houses. Mr Manning, I really think you should consider coming back, I think you need to sort this out yourself."

Manning cut him short. "Look, it's Friday now, if I leave straight after my race on Sunday and drive through the night, I can be in the office first thing Monday morning. By then, things might have died down a bit, and it will give me time to think. In the meantime, I'll try and get hold of Harrison on his private number." He rang off.

Derek Harrison's phone went to voicemail. Manning didn't leave a message.

Howard Fryer had stepped away when Manning's phone rang. Whatever the boss had to talk about, he wasn't interested. His was a world dominated by brake horsepower and g forces he didn't know anything about planning applications or building regulations. So long as his employer had enough money to pay the bills, he wasn't bothered.

Manning walked the couple of paces to where Fryer was standing. He stood silently for twenty or thirty seconds, then asked if the car was ready.

"Yes, it's ready to go. Practice starts in half an hour. I'll get the boys back, you get changed and we'll warm the car up."

Manning emerged from the transporter fifteen minutes later wearing his race suit and carrying his crash helmet in it's protective bag. The noise from the big V8 engine rose and fell as the mechanic blipped the accelerator. Manning took his helmet from the bag and put it on.

Andy and Susan were sitting in the small living room of their apartment trying to settle down after the excitement of the morning's planning meeting. Settling down was not going to be easy, the continued ringing of the telephone would not allow it.

"You know what?" Andy said. "I might as well open the shop, at least that way we'll be away from all these phone calls. Who knows, we might even make a bit of money. We could do with it."

They went together. The shop looked the same. They somehow imagined that with all that had gone on the last three days, the shop would be different, but it wasn't. At the moment it was the only stability in their lives. A sanctuary away from the chaos caused by Victor Manning.

They busied themselves checking the stock. They had a policy of moving things around so the shop always looked different. There was nothing worse than an antique shop with stock that never moved. As they worked, customers came and browsed, buying the odd piece here and there. Nothing too significant but all sales were greatly appreciated.

In their minds they knew the visits from the hired thugs were a thing of the past but neither of them found it easy. Every time a vehicle parked outside the shop they tensed mentally, Andy instinctively stepping between Susan and the door. Most of their customers lived modest lives, they dressed casually and in the most part drove modest nondescript cars. This was not Bond Street. So, when a late model Mercedes coupe pulled up outside it was immediately noticed.

Andy joked,"We don't get many customers driving Mercs. we could be all-right here, Su."

A smartly dressed lady walked through the door. Probably in her fifties, with a nice figure and fragrant perfume, she knew how to look after herself and, if appearances were anything to go by, she had the money to pay for it.

"Hello. Please feel free to look around. If there is anything special you want or if we can help, just ask. My name is Susan and this is my partner, Andy."

Although outwardly confident, the customer gave the impression that she was somehow uncomfortable in the antiques shop.

"I hope you don't think I'm being foolish but I've never been in an antiques shop before. I've passed here many times and looked through the windows, but I've never had the nerve to come in. You see, I know nothing about antiques, I'm not even sure what a real antique is. That must sound really silly to you."

Andy smiled at her and she rather nervously smiled back.

"Well, technically an antique is around one hundred years old but we're not too precise here. If it's old and you like it, that's good enough reason to buy it. We can generally give you an idea of age and of course, if it's silver or gold it will have a dated assay stamp."

"Oh, I'm learning already, I didn't know silver or gold is dated."

Andy knew exactly what he was doing, the more you talk to someone who is a little nervous, the more you are able to make them feel at ease, and if you are able to make them like you, there is a very fair chance you can make a sale.

"We'll leave you to have a look around, but we love our work and we are both very happy to talk about anything in the shop. Please don't feel obliged to buy, we really are happy to talk."

The customer spent upwards of fifteen minutes checking most of the stock before asking Susan, "I think I might like to start a small collection of something interesting. I have several friends who collect china dolls and things like that, but to be honest that is not really my thing. Have you any suggestions?"

"Have you thought about silver thimbles? They will have assay stamps or hallmarks, as they are known so you can accurately date them. There are lots of different designs and when you look at them, you can imagine they have been used repeatedly over the past hundred years or so. I don't mean to be rude but they are relatively cheap, so you could build up a nice collection for not too much money, and we always have several in stock."

"Do you know what? That sounds absolutely perfect. Show me what you have" Ten minutes later, the customer left with the beginnings of her collection. Five Victorian thimbles. "Thanks for your help, I'll definitely be back."

"We'll look forward to seeing you again. Thimbles and sewing items are among our specialities; we're sure to have more stock in a few days."

That Friday afternoon, the time spent in the shop was like a tonic to Andy and Susan. They were able to forget the horrors of the past three days, forget about Victor Manning, and concentrate on their own lives.

The ground was shaking, the noise was deafening, several million pounds' worth of historic racing cars were lined up, waiting for the track officials to indicate the start of practice. Somewhere in the mass of cars was Manning's bright red Ford Mustang. The cars were released row by row. By the time the Mustang was waved off, the first cars were clear of the La Source hairpin and were heading down towards Eau Rouge and onto the fastest part of the track. Manning tried to clear his mind. He'd done this a hundred times before, but never when he was facing bankruptcy and ruin. He knew he could fight it, he knew he could win just as he knew he could win this motor race. What he didn't need was any thoughts of self-doubt.

He felt good driving the Mustang. The dashboard instruments confirmed what he instinctively knew, the car was running perfectly. There was no better prepared car on the race track. He moved up through the gears, threading between the slower cars, cursing those that got in his way.

Through Eau Rouge and onto the Kemmel Straight, one of the fastest parts of the circuit. He had no time to think about his problems back in England, now, today, he was Victor Manning, racing driver, and on Sunday he would be Victor Manning, race winner, hero to the fans applauding his victory. For now, he concentrated on the job in hand. Lap after lap he drove round, gradually getting faster. He was making mental notes about the track, where there was a dip or a bump, where there might be a problem with grip or where it might be possible to overtake. All the things that would make a difference between winning and losing. When he felt he had completed enough laps to know every detail about the track, he turned off the circuit and into the pits. Howard Fryer was waiting for him.

"The car looked and sounded good. Are you happy with it?"

"Yeah, Howard, you and the lads have done a superb job as always. No problems at all. You look after the car, get it ready for qualifying tomorrow, I've got a few things to sort out. I'm going to get changed then go back to the hotel."

"Okay boss, we'll be ready for tomorrow. Qualifying starts at ten. We'll see you then."

Manning got changed in the race transporter. Fryer was casually checking over the car when he came out.

"Howard, the boys did a good job. Take them out for a drink later." As he turned to leave, he tucked a hundred euros into Fryer's pocket.

"Thanks, Mr Manning. When Manning was out of earshot, Fryer shouted to the others in the team. "Blimey, that's a first. Drinks on the governor boys."

Back at the hotel, Manning sat in the bar. Not *at* the bar as he would normally do, but in a quiet corner with a brandy and his mobile phone on the table in front of him.

At Telcote Manor, the telephone was ringing. Asli m lady in her fifties answered it.

"Oh Hello, I didn't expect to hear from you, you don't normally ring. Is everything alright?"

"Yes, I'm fine, but there are a couple of issues."

"A couple of issues? What sort of issues?"

"Look, if the newspapers should come knocking on the door, just stay quiet and say you know nothing about it."

"Well, I don't know anything about it, whatever it is. You're scaring me. Just tell me what's going on."

"The shit has really hit the fan…"

"You know I don't like you using that sort of language." She interrupted.

"Well, there is no other expression to use. My latest planning application has been thrown out and there is a vendetta against me from all quarters. So, whatever happens and whoever calls, just say you don't know anything."

"Well, I won't be lying, I don't know. Mainly because you never talk to me."

"Don't start all that now, I've got enough on my plate. Look, I'm leaving right after the race on Sunday. I should be home early Monday morning. I'll explain then."

He rang off.

She carried on polishing the shelf and arranging her silver thimbles.

Next, he called his secretary.

"Mr Manning, everything is going mad here. We've had reporters outside the door all morning. The local radio station has been on the phone asking for an interview and we have emails from housing associations and solicitors representing disgruntled buyers. No one here knows what to tell them."

"I was hoping that things might have settled down since I spoke to Seymour earlier but obviously that's not the case. Look, get Seymour to check how many claims buyers have made about the houses before today. If we don't have any historical claims, then anything mentioned after today won't have much relevance, will it? Also get him to check if any of the housing association homes have been sold on to private buyers. If they have, then the onus is on the buyer's surveyors to detect any faults. I know I'm clutching at straws, but I'm turning myself inside out trying to save the business and all your jobs."

"Mr Manning, you know all the staff will do everything they can to help," She added, not very convincingly.

"Angela, whatever you do, keep all this under your hat. Don't breathe a word to anyone outside the office. It's late Friday afternoon now. I'll be in the office Monday morning."

He rang off and drained the brandy in one flowing move. He slid back into his chair, the warm feeling that only alcohol can provide creeping over him.

"Another one of these over here, love."

The girl behind the bar turned away from him and cursed under her breath. "I'm not your love!"

She took her time pouring the brandy but there is a limit on how long you can stall and still be in the realms of good service. When she was ready, she took the drink over to his table.

Manning looked up at her. "My phone calls didn't bother you, did they? It's just a few business issues that needed sorting. You know what it's like, if you're the boss, there's always something you have to do. You can't rely on your staff to do anything right. I'm sure you understand."

She did not. He carried on regardless.

"Is the restaurant good here? I'm starving."

"Yes sir, it's very good."

"Are you working all evening? I must get something to eat now but we could continue our conversation afterwards."

He didn't give her a chance to reply. He drank the brandy and walked the short distance to the restaurant.

Two hours later, Manning returned to the bar. He smiled at her as he walked back to the same table he was sitting at before.

"I'm racing tomorrow, I better not drink too much, but I could have another brandy when you are ready, love. You are not very busy here. Would you like to join me?"

"I'm not some sort of hostess at a club. I'm not allowed to sit with customers."

She quickly left his drink on the table and returned to the bar.

Talking to members of the opposite sex was not something Victor Manning was good at. He was used to telling people what to do and if they didn't like it, they knew the alternative. But here was a young, feisty woman talking to him as if he was a little child. In some sort of subconscious way, she aroused him. He was a long way from home, no one knew him, he had no onlookers, no one to judge or snigger at him. He waited a few minutes to let her settle behind the bar then he approached her.

"Look, I'm sorry. I didn't intend to embarrass you and I definitely didn't mean to suggest anything improper. I'm over here on my own and I'm a bit lonely. Would it be okay if I sat here and talked to you?"

"Yes sir, that would be alright. But if I get busy I have to attend to the other customers."

"Of course, I understand that. Let me introduce myself. My name is Victor. I'm racing at the Spa track this weekend. What is your name?"

She really did not want to get dragged into conversation with this man. She had already decided she didn't like him, but he was a guest and indirectly he paid her wages, so she had little choice. She was clear in her mind that she would not be more friendly than her job demanded.

"My name is Lina."

"That's a nice name, I don't think I know anyone else with the same name."

"It's quite common here in Belgium."

For an hour or so they made small talk. Lina kept her distance during the conversations, she stayed aloof. But as they spoke, she realised that after her initial outburst at Manning's table, the tone of the conversation had changed. Instead of being a demanding customer, Manning was changing into a submissive boy hanging onto her every word. She still didn't like him, but she knew a little boy would not present her with any problems when it was time to close the bar.

"Lina, I'll try one more brandy please, I'm sure that won't make any difference to my performance, I mean my performance tomorrow at the race circuit." He giggled.

As she turned her back on him to fill the glass, she muttered under her breath, "Don't worry about your performance, you will always be a loser."

For Lina the evening dragged on. She served a few other customers but the hotel wasn't busy and the bar was virtually empty. She was bored, she wanted to go home. Manning was the only thing keeping her from going home and going to bed.

On the stroke of midnight, she told Manning that her shift was over and the bar was closing. He sat and watched her as she went through the routine of shutting down. He tried to talk to her but she pretended not to hear as she cleared up.

She thought to herself, *'For God's sake, what's wrong with this man? Why won't he leave me alone?'* Her thoughts were in direct contrast to Manning's. He had never managed to hold a conversation with a woman over an entire evening, even if it was one-sided. The brandy had given him false confidence. In his own inflated mind, he thought he had a chance with Lina.

"I have to go now, sir," she said without any ambiguity.

"It's dark out there, I'll walk you to your car."

"There really is no need, the car park is well lit and I have a headache. I need some quiet time."

"No, I insist. I've enjoyed our evening together. If you don't mind, I consider it my duty to see you safely to your car."

"Very well, but there is no need."

They walked out of the hotel together and across the car park. She stopped next to a small Citroen. "This is my car. You see, I am perfectly safe, but thank you anyway. "She pressed the remote and opened the door.

It wasn't particularly warm but Manning was sweating. He was excited. He moved closer to her.

"Goodnight Lina. We've had a good chat tonight, haven't we? We've really got to know one another. A goodnight kiss would end a perfect evening for me, and it might bring me luck for the race."

"Please sir, Mr Manning, Victor, I am a bartender and you are a customer, nothing more. Now please, I just want to go home, I'm very tired."

"Lina! Don't be like that, I thought we had made a connection during the evening. Surely one little kiss wouldn't hurt."

"I have just said no. Now please leave me alone."

Manning was gripping her left arm. She was trying to get into the car but she couldn't free herself from his grip.

"Lina. I don't understand, we enjoyed each other's company. I can't believe you are saying these things."

Manning tightened his grip on her arm and pulled her around so that they stood face to face. He moved forward in a clumsy attempt to kiss her. She tried to spin her head around but he forced his lips on hers. She threw her head left and right but he moved his hands to hold her still.

He was not used to resistance. It had been a long time since he had touched his wife in that way and his secretary knew what he wanted and was happy to provide it, for a price. Now he was like a submissive puppy dog that nudged and scratched its owner until it was stroked. In his mind he was that puppy and it was a game she was playing, any minute she would respond and he would get his reward.

It was no game for Lina. His hands were everywhere, holding her face, squeezing her body, grabbing at her breasts.

She reacted the only way she knew, she brought her knee up into his crotch. For a split second he released his hold on her. It was enough time for her to enter the car through the open door, slam it shut and lock it. She sat there sobbing, too frightened to move. She managed to compose herself enough to put the keys in the ignition and start the engine. She slammed the car into gear and roared off, the wheels spinning on the loose gravel.

Manning was still standing there, looking at her driving away. He didn't get it. He didn't understand what he had done wrong. He'd been polite and, attentive, he'd talked to her nicely. Why did she have to get all prim and proper over it? After all, she was only a barmaid. He went into the hotel and back to his room.

He didn't dwell on what had happened. The evening's events weren't going to change anything. In the morning he had to complete his qualifying laps, and on Sunday he had a race that he could win. When he returned to the hotel tomorrow, he would check that Lina was feeling better and hope they could carry on as if nothing unpleasant had happened.

He fell into a deep sleep. He didn't hear the knocking on his door until it rose to a furious banging. "Okay. Okay. I'm coming. What time is it, for God's sake?"

He opened the bedroom door to see two police officers standing there, one male, one female. They both had their hands resting on their holstered pistols.

"Mr Victor Manning, you must come with us now."

"What's this all about? Give me a few minutes to wake up properly and put some clothes on."

"You must come now."

The two police officers worked as a well-rehearsed team. As the burly policeman spun Manning around, his female colleague snapped the handcuffs on his wrists.

"Look, officers, what is all this about? You can see I'm only wearing my pants. At least let me get dressed."

"You'll find out at the police station; you'll have your chance when we get there. Now be quiet."

He was bundled out of the hotel and into the rear of a waiting police car. He barely had time to sit on the seat before the car started and drove quickly away. For once in his life, Victor Manning was lost for words, but for the second time in two days, bad things were happening to him and he did not like it.

At the police station he was roughly dragged out of the car and frogmarched into the building and through a maze of corridors. Finally, a door at the end of a dark and depressing corridor was opened and he was pushed in, still handcuffed and still only wearing his pants. As the police officers left, he heard the chilling sound of the door being locked. He was cold and frightened. He had no phone, no identification and no clothes, and he didn't know why he was there. With his hands behind his back he couldn't see the expensive watch he always wore so he had no way of knowing what time it was. Whatever was happening, he had no alternative but to wait until someone explained or apologised. He guessed it was over an hour ago that the police came for him. Surely it wouldn't take much longer for them to realise their mistake and let him go. He was desperate to sleep and wake up to find it had all been a bad dream. But the cold and fear wouldn't let him sleep, and it was not a bad dream. This was happening.

Time passed so slowly but eventually he thought he could see a beam of light beneath the door. A few minutes later, the door opened and light flooded the room. Manning had to blink and rub his eyes to get them accustomed to the brightness. Two large men walked in. One of them held a plastic cup, which he placed in front of Manning; the other man reached behind and unlocked the handcuffs.

"A cup of Belgian police tea for you, Mr Manning. Probably not up to the standard of your usual Earl Grey, but it's the best we can do."

"Look, What is all this about?I was dragged here in the middle of the night, I'm practically naked and freezing cold, and I'm supposed to be at the race circuit in an hour or so."

The two detectives opened a thin folder with a few pages inside.

"Can you tell us what happened last evening, Mr Manning?"

"I don't know what you mean. Nothing happened. I had a meal in the hotel restaurant, a few drinks in the bar and then I went to bed."

"What time did you eat in the restaurant?"

"I think about seven p.m. I wasn't very hungry. I think I left about an hour later."

"Then what did you do?"

"I went upstairs to my room to freshen up, then I went down to the bar. I stayed there talking to Lina, that's the barmaid, until midnight when I went to bed."

"Mr Manning, we have just returned from searching your hotel room. Our experts have just finished checking your computer. They found that you were online between seven minutes past eight o'clock and twelve minutes past nine. What were you looking at?"

"Nothing in particular, just some business stuff, maybe a news website. I can't remember everything I looked at."

"Did you look at pornography?"

"No. Definitely not. Well, not on purpose. Sometimes these sites pop up by accident, you know how it is."

"No. Mr Manning, we do not know how it is. Our experts found that you looked at five different pornographic sites in that period."

"Well, maybe I did, it's not easy keeping an accurate check on what you are doing. Anyway, they were all legal, nothing against the law."

"Mr Manning, we think that these porno websites…"he hesitated "…shall we say, stirred up your sexual frustration, which led you to attack the young lady working behind the bar."

"No, that's not true. We were flirting with each other all evening; it was a game. She was playing hard to get and I was going along with it. What has she been saying?"

"Mr Manning, we have the girl's statement that you tried to force yourself on her. You assaulted her in a sexual manner with intent to rape her."

"No! That is not how it happened at all. We enjoyed each other's company all evening and I just wanted to give her a goodnight kiss."

"Mr Manning let's stop messing around. We have the girl's statement backed up by the images captured on the closed-circuit surveillance camera covering the car park. I am afraid you will not be racing this weekend, and possibly not for a long time. We will give you some clothes to wear while we carry out a thorough search of your room and your car. In the meantime, you will be held in a police cell and you will appear before magistrates on Monday."

"Whatever you think you saw on the closed-circuit screen, that's not how it happened. You and that girl will be sorry you ever made these accusations. Can I please have my phone so that I can contact my mechanics, who are waiting for me at the track? I also need to contact my wife."

"No! Your cell phone will be examined by our technical experts, however, we will allow the use of our telephone for one call only."

The two detectives picked up the folder and left the room. Manning wasn't alone for very long. A young policeman entered the room carrying a dark grey tracksuit jacket and leggings. He threw the clothes at Manning and, in a heavy

Belgian accent, told him to put them on. He also tossed a well-used mobile phone on the table.

"One call."

Manning picked up the clothes and started to get dressed.

"Have these ever been washed? They smell of cigarettes and sweat."

It was a wasted question. The policeman ignored him. Manning picked up the phone. He wondered who he should call. It was still early in the morning; his wife would be in bed, but Howard Fryer and the other mechanics would be up and ready. He realised that he wasn't expected home until Monday morning. He was hoping this would all be sorted by then. He called Fryer.

"Howard, look, something really big and unexpected has cropped up. I'm not going to be able to race. Can you and the boys pack things up and return home?"

"Yeah, of course we can. This is totally unexpected. Is there anything we can do for you? Are you alright?"

"Yeah, I'm sort of alright. There's nothing you can do, thanks. I've got to sort this out for myself."

"Okay boss, if you are sure you're alright we'll load up the car and make our way home. We'll make contact later. Cheers for now."

Manning finished the call and handed the phone back to the officer. The policeman led him out of the interview room and ultimately into a cell. The door closed chillingly behind him.

TWENTY-EIGHT

On Saturday morning, Andy and Susan rose early. They were desperate to get their lives back on track and put the events of the past few weeks behind them. For Andy, the situation wasn't quite so simple. He knew the police would want witness statements and that would probably mean appearing in court; he also knew that he, and particularly Susan, might still be targeted by gang members looking for revenge or trying to influence their evidence. He could handle that. He wasn't too worried for his own safety, he knew he could look after himself, but it was different for Susan. She was an innocent bystander in all that had gone on. She had already suffered enough, and he knew it was all because of him.

He could only imagine what might have gone through her mind in that awful warehouse. He made a silent promise to himself that whatever might happen in the future, he would always be there to protect her.

He kept his thoughts and worries to himself. He knew that Susan was still troubled and it would take time for her to settle down. The only way he knew to restore her inner peace was to carry on as if nothing had happened. If at any time in the future she wanted to talk about her feelings and fears, he would be there for her, but for now he would do his best to return to their old life.

When they were ready, they left the flat and drove to their shop. Saturdays were often their busiest day but business was slower than normal and by mid-morning they had the chance to sit down with a cup of coffee.

After a long pause, Susan said to Andy, "You know that lady who bought the thimbles yesterday? Well, I think I know her. I think she is Victor Manning's wife. I thought she looked familiar when I first saw her, but I was embarrassed to say anything with all that has been going on. I didn't want to say the wrong thing. I only met her once, at the completion of one of his housing developments about twenty years ago. I'm sure it's her."

Andy thought for a moment, then replied, "You know, I had a similar feeling. I saw a faded newspaper article in the bottom of a drawer I was clearing. There was a photo of you and your husband and Manning and her. To be honest, I only looked at you and didn't pay any attention to the other people; at that time, they didn't mean anything to me. But I did think you were a looker and I still do."

"I'm not sure if that is a compliment or not. But I'll take it as one."

They both allowed themselves a little giggle.

Andy's face took a serious turn. "You don't suppose there was anything behind her visit, do you? She's not part of some sort of plot? Frankly, after what's been going on, I wouldn't put anything past that man."

"I don't think so. From what I can remember she was unconcerned about her husband and his work. As I recall, on the day of the photograph she hardly spoke to him. I do remember that he went off to talk to the press and she sat in the car on her own. I thought it strange at the time. She has lost a bit of weight since then which is why I didn't recognise her straightaway. And of course, it was a long time ago."

Andy turned and glanced towards the door.

"Well, now's our chance to ask her. She's just parked the Merc."

Susan greeted her, "Hello again. Excuse me if I'm wrong, but you are Mrs Manning, aren't you? I didn't immediately recognise you yesterday. It was only later when I thought about it that I realised you were familiar to me."

"Yes I am, but I'm sorry, I don't recognise you."

"I'm Susan Harrison, Derek's wife. Well, estranged wife now. We posed together with our husbands for a newspaper photograph about twenty years ago."

"Yes, that sounds vaguely familiar. I really don't have anything to do with my husband's work but I did get dragged into posing for a couple of pictures. Victor never talks to me about business, but I do read the newspapers and I know he has had some bad publicity because of some involvement with an antiques dealer. Oh! My goodness! I've just realised… is that you or your partner?"

Andy interrupted her. "I'm afraid it was me and I hate to say it, but what you have read is only the tip of the iceberg. There will be a lot more in the press soon. If it makes any difference to things, Susan had nothing to do with any of my actions except that she took the full force of your husband's plan to silence me."

Now it was Susan's turn to butt in. "Mrs Manning, I'm sorry to confront you like this but I totally and fully stand by what Andy has done. To be honest, I think he is a public hero and I can't tell you how proud I am of him."

If Mrs Manning was surprised, she didn't show it.

"Look, I know my husband is no saint but believe me, I don't know anything about his business dealings. In the very early days he used to tell me what was going on, but these last twenty years or more he hasn't told me anything; in fact, we barely speak. All I know is that at the moment, he is abroad somewhere, racing that blasted car. Susan, you said you were separated from your husband. I suspect that we are both casualties of our husband's success."

"Or greed," Susan added.

Andy entered the conversation. "Look, as I see it, Su's life with her husband was over before I met her and it seems to me, Mrs Manning, that you lead a separate life to your husband. Me, I'm stuck somewhere in the middle. Susan and I have fallen head over heels in love with one another, and with regards to me and your husband, I just happened to be someone who cared and who was in the wrong place at the wrong time. End of. Anyway, forgetting all that, if you have come back as a satisfied customer, you are very welcome."

"Andy, Susan, I like you both, you make a good couple and, may I say it, a very professional partnership. And before things go any further, my name is Penelope, everyone calls me Penny. The main reason I came to the shop today was to thank you for those lovely little thimbles and the advice you gave me. I know it sounds a bit silly, but I cleared a space on a shelf and set the thimbles in a display with a spotlight shining on them, and they look super. I never realised something so small could cheer me up so much. I know it sounds like a cliché, but I really don't go out a great deal and the ladies

I do meet are all married to doctors or accountants and, despite the fact that my husband provides very well for me, they regard me as beneath them as I'm married to a builder, even if he is a wealthy builder. So, it was a breath of fresh air meeting and talking to you two. I have a photo of the thimbles on my phone, let me show you."

She found the picture on her phone and showed it to Susan. The photo showed a polished mahogany shelf with the thimbles standing on small, crocheted doilies that hung over the edge to form a delicate fringe, all illuminated by an overhead spotlight.

"Penny, the thimbles look amazing. If you don't mind me saying so, you have a wonderful eye for detail. You have made something so small and simple into an eye-catching display; you obviously have a flair for it. I can see the rest of the room in the background and that also looks beautiful. Are you responsible for all the interior design in your home or do you get designers in?"

"No designers. I do it all myself. I like going around the charity shops and picking up bits and pieces. That's where the doilies came from."

Andy glanced across to Susan. "We could do with some of your artistic flair in our shop. We just throw the goods out; sometimes I think we might make more money if we had the time and ability to create a set theme, like a corner of a lounge or bedroom or something like that."

Penny's eyes lit up and a smile crept over her face.

"I could do that for you. Oh! Please let me! I would absolutely love to do it. I don't want payment or anything like that. Oh! Please!" She was like a little girl pleading for a puppy dog.

Susan and Andy were taken by surprise. The general idea was something they had talked over between themselves many times. Small, specialised items were normally sold to collectors who know what they are looking for, but buyers of larger items like tables, bookcases and cabinets were often undecided because they couldn't imagine them in their own house. A large display might give them the confidence to make a purchase. On the other side of the argument, trade buyers like to rummage through stacked shelves and boxes in the hope of finding a forgotten gem. But of course, there are no forgotten gems. No antiques shop is ever going to sell anything without having first checked it out and tried to establish the correct price. But most trade buyers live in hope. Maybe they could have two shops in one, a carefully laid out display in the window and an Aladdin's cave of treasure in the main body of the shop. The idea made a lot of sense.

Susan made the first suggestion. "Penny, using whatever we have in the shop, could you make a little display in our window, maybe using some of the larger bits we have had in stock for some time?"

"I could definitely do that. I might need some help grouping things of the same age together but otherwise I don't think it would be a problem."

Andy had been deep in thought. "Penny, these ideas do sound very good and I think it would help sales in the shop, but – and it's a big but – we don't really have the money to pay you."

Penny looked shocked. "I don't need any payment. I would be happy doing it for nothing."

Su interrupted. "Andy and Penny, look, we have lots of stock that has sat around for ages. Why don't we let Penny do her display and if the idea works, we might be able to sell this old stock at a higher price than we would otherwise have done. If we do, then Penny can keep the difference."

Penny stopped her. "Look, I don't want any money, I don't need it. If we manage to make more, I would like it to go to charity."

Andy and Susan looked at each other, then at Penny. Andy said, "That sounds like a plan. Let's give it a try."

The three of them chatted away like excited schoolchildren, swapping ideas and suggestions. Ever aware of the customers coming through the door, one of them had to break off every so often to make a sale or answer a query. By the end of the morning, they had talked through all the possible benefits of Penny's idea.

Andy finalised things by saying, "We have a lot of old stock in store at the back of the shop – why don't you go and have a look to see what you can use? If anything needs a polish or maybe something more, just let me know. We'll do the manual work; you just use your creativity. When do you want to start?"

"I'll have a quick look now if that's alright, then that gives me tomorrow to design a display and I'll come back on Monday morning and make a start. My husband should be back some time on Monday, not that it makes any difference. He'll have a surprise when I tell him I've got a job!"

"He'll have a surprise right enough when you tell him you're working here."

On Saturday morning in the small town of Spa in eastern Belgium, Victor Manning was lying on his bed in the police station cell. He hadn't slept all night. He was confused, frightened, cold and hungry. The door opened. In the split second it took for someone to open the door and walk through, Manning hoped that it might be one of the police officers he had seen last night. But this was another face. Obviously the other policemen had changed shifts. He was thinking that at least he had some connection to the officers he had previously seen and spoken to, but to a new face, he was just another prisoner.

"Here is a cup of tea and a sandwich. Don't take too long eating as you are going before the magistrate in thirty minutes."

"The magistrate! Look, this is silly, all I did was make a pass at the girl. The girl and you have got it all wrong."

"The girl, as you described her, was trying to go home after a long shift. Not only did you stop her doing that, you tried to force your attention on her. You touched her improperly. Luckily for you she managed to escape, otherwise you would be facing a very serious charge indeed. No more talk. We must go now."

Manning was escorted out of the cell through a maze of corridors. Once outside the building, he was roughly pushed into a police van, waiting with the engine running. The driver didn't wait for him to get settled, nor did the other prisoners inside the van. Before Manning had a chance to sit down, the vehicle sped off. The other occupants crowded round him.

"So, you're the rich English pervert who tried to rape one of our girls. We heard all about you. You were the talk of the station, this rich English racing driver. You thought you could get away with it, did you? You better pray that you get bail, otherwise you will end up someone's bitch in jail. See how you'll like that."

Manning had no idea who he was sharing the van with. There were three of them. Obviously they were all local and had been in the police station overnight. He guessed they might have been drunks or in a scuffle somewhere. In truth, they looked like some of his workers back in England. He had never been so scared in his life. He didn't know how far away the magistrates' court was. He did not know how long he would be sharing the small space in the van with them, and he didn't know what would happen if they decided to kick off.

He didn't have to wait long.

The largest of the three moved over and sat on the bench next to Manning.

"Mr English Racing Driver, what time is it?"

Manning was surprised. Why would they want to know the time? Without a second thought, he looked at his watch. Wrong move.

"Look at that watch! It must be worth a small fortune. I've lifted a few of those; it must be at least five thousand euros." They all burst out laughing, except Manning.

"Mr Racing Driver, why don't you give it to me for safekeeping?"

Manning tried to edge away. "I think it will be okay, it hasn't come to any harm yet." He tried to make light of it.

"You don't understand. If you give me your watch, it will be you that will be safe." More laughter.

Manning had been in tight scrapes before but he was no street fighter; he always had someone else to do it for him. But he was in no mood to hand over his watch.

"Look, I don't want any trouble. This is all a big mistake. When the magistrate hears all the facts, I'll be away from here and on my way home." He was trying to buy himself some time, hoping that the magistrates' court wasn't too far away."

When they realised that Manning wasn't an easy touch they backed off, but that didn't stop them threatening him for the rest of the journey. It seemed like hours to Manning but in fact the journey was soon over. The van stopped and the officers opened the door. Manning was the first up on his feet. As he stood near the door, the large prisoner he had previously tangled with stood up quickly and shoulder-charged him, sending him crashing out of the vehicle and falling onto the concrete below.

"Mr Racing Driver, you are so clumsy," he taunted as the others laughed.

Manning picked himself up, his tracksuit leggings ripped and his hands grazed and bleeding. The police officers looked on, unconcerned. One by one, the three occupants of the van climbed out and all of them were led through a back door and into a holding room with wooden benches lining two opposite walls. Between the benches was a large polished door with ornate brass fittings. Manning assumed that this door led to the courtroom.

A policeman came in with them and stood silently, his arms folded in front of his chest, his face not showing any emotion. Not looking left or right. For fifteen minutes they sat in silence, then the polished door opened and a short, overweight lady walked in. She spoke to the four of them in French. Manning had no idea what she said.

Before she turned and walked away, he tried to catch her attention. "Madame, *excuse moi!*" But his bad schoolboy French didn't stop her from walking away.

His antagonist was quick to carry on. "What's the matter, Mr Racing Driver? Doesn't she listen? You're not in England now. Try speaking French, *n'est ce pas!*" More laughter.

The door closed and opened again seconds later. This time, a policeman ushered them into the courtroom. The four defendants were lined up together in a dark wooden-panelled, glass-fronted cage. Manning didn't know what was going on. He couldn't understand French and the court either could not or would not speak English. He realised that the three people in front of him appeared to be giving their names and addresses, so when his turn came, he tried to follow suit.

"I am Victor Manning, a British citizen. I demand you speak in English."

The magistrate appeared to ignore him. With his lack of understanding of the French language, Manning didn't know what was going on, but to him it appeared that the three Belgians were all charged with the same offence. When the magistrate finished speaking, they all smiled and slapped each other on the back, and before walking out, turned and winked at him. They didn't have to say anything. The wink said it all.

The magistrate addressed Manning. "Mr Manning, I have been told that you do not understand French, so as a courtesy I will address you in English."

Manning replied, "Thank you, I appreciate that."

The magistrate continued, "You have been charged with sexual assault. Fortunately, there is no evidence of violence on your part; however, it is a very serious offence. Your case will be heard by a judge and jury, when you will be able to submit any mitigating evidence. Until your case is heard,

I have the authority to remand you in jail or to grant your temporary freedom, provided you surrender your passport."

The magistrate turned to his clerk and had a short conversation in French. He then turned back to talk to Manning.

"Mr Manning, you will surrender your passport to the police station, you will report to the police station each day, you may not leave the town of Spa, and you will not make any attempt to speak to the victim of your crime. Do you understand?"

Manning meekly replied, "Yes, sir."

The court official led him by the arm out of the dock, through the polished door and into the waiting police van for the journey back to the police station. Once there, the officers returned all his property, which they had previously taken from the hotel, including his car keys but not his computer.

"We have moved your car. It is now in our car park, You are entitled to use it but remember, you cannot leave the area. You must report here every day at six p.m. You will be informed when you will be required to attend court. Do not try to contact the girl in any way. For your sake, do not return to the hotel. Find an alternative place to stay. Do you understand?"

"Yes, I understand. Thank you."

On Monday morning, Andy and Sue found Penny waiting outside the shop. Andy smiled as he opened the door.

"My goodness, you are keen!"

"You know what they say – a new broom sweeps clean! Now, when I looked on Saturday, I found a few interesting bits in your storeroom and I've thought of a couple of ideas for a window display. If you could give me a hand to get them out, I'll explain what I have in mind."

Andy helped Penny retrieve the old stock and between them they cleaned off the dust and cobwebs. Next, they cleared a space in the overcrowded window. All the time Susan had run the shop on her own, she had never had time to arrange the window in any sort of display worth the name. She had been too busy buying and researching new stock; even after Andy had joined her, their time was split between buying and selling, and more recently, a lot of time was lost thanks to Victor Manning. Hopefully that period of their lives was over and they could start looking forward to their own future.

They never paid too much attention to what Penny was doing. There were plenty of other things to be getting on with, but during the morning they happened to look out of the front of the shop to see a small group of three or four people looking through the window. They were pointing and moving their heads in an attempt to get a better look at what was being displayed.

"Crikey, we've not had an audience before," Andy remarked to Su.

When they looked, Penny had transformed the shop window into what could be imagined as an old country gentleman's study. A well-used wooden armchair sat behind a heavily stained oak desk. On the desk, an old brass Anglepoise lamp sat next to a wire letter rack. A carved wooden pen holder with a handful of old pens and pencils stood to one side; on the other, an old cup with no handle held two well-loved pipes. Several heavily framed paintings hung on the wall, showing scenes of shire horses, dogs, cattle and other country pursuits.

None of these items had any merit on their own: the chair was well used and showing signs of bad repair, the table was badly scratched and bearing several cup rings. In short, all the pieces were such that individually, you would not look at them twice, but collectively and displayed as they were they looked exactly like every person's image of an old man's office.

Penny continued to add little touches here and there. A cigarette lighter next to the pipes. An old pair of glasses casually left in the middle. A bone-handled penknife with a broken blade laying near the pen rack.

The display continued to provide an attraction for the window gazers. When Penny was satisfied that she had done all she could with the items that were available to her, she left her work and joined Andy and Susan.

Susan couldn't contain herself. "Penny, I think that looks brilliant! And judging by the people looking through the window, they think so too. It's amazing that those old bits and pieces were basically rubbish on their own, but they look superb in a setting like that. All we want now is for someone to buy something."

While Susan and Penny chatted to each other, Andy walked out of the shop to get a pavement view of the display. As he stood and admired Penny's work he was aware of a lady standing next to him. After a brief casual glance, he turned to go back into the shop. As he turned, he realised the lady was paying particular attention to the layout and looking at it from every angle.

Sensing the possibility of a sale, Andy asked if she liked it and if there was anything he could help her with.

"Yes. As it happens, there might be. Can I come in and talk to you about it?"

"Of course, please come in. I'm Andy and these are my partners, Susan and Penny."

Andy didn't know how he should introduce Penny; she wasn't strictly a partner in any sense of the word. Neither was she an employee. For now, partner would have to do.

The lady introduced herself. "My name is Naome and in the technical sense, I'm here to put a business proposition to you."

"Sounds interesting," Su replied.

"I'm an independent props advisor to the film industry and right now, I'm working on a film that desperately needs a set display exactly as you have created here. We've tried working with what we've got and frankly, it's just not happening."

Andy grasped the situation. "Give me a minute or two and I'll give you a price for all the items."

"No. I don't want to buy them, that's not how the industry works. If we bought everything we use, we would need an aircraft hangar to store stuff that we might only use once. I want to hire the entire display for about a month. When we have finished with it, you can have it back. I assume that you haven't done this type of thing before. It can be quite lucrative for you, and if you can deliver and collect it when we're finished, it will be extremely useful to us. Making movies is our business, that's what we do. Anything that enables us to work efficiently and quickly is amply rewarded. Can you deliver to our location? We're filming in a farmhouse in the Peak District."

"Yes, no problems there."

"I am happy to authorise a payment of one thousand

pounds for four weeks' hire. If we should run over, any extra days would be pro-rata."

Andy looked at Susan. They both managed to hide their surprise, which was not easy as they would have been happy to sell the lot for less than half that figure.

Naome produced a headed notepad from her handbag and proceeded to write down the delivery address.

"Please deliver first thing tomorrow. I'll have an official order waiting for you and we'll let you know when you can collect."

They exchanged telephone numbers and she left.

Andy, Susan and Penny looked at each other. Susan broke the silence.

"Well, that's pretty good for a first morning at work. What are you going to do after lunch?"

They all enjoyed the moment. None of them could believe what had just happened.

"Penny, that is a brilliant deal and it's all down to you. Without your design expertise, that would never have happened. I hope these old bits are really what they want. I guess we'll know this time tomorrow". Andy was interrupted by the ringing of a cell phone. Penny reached into her pocket and looked at her phone.

"Sorry, it's my husband. I really should take this."

She held the small phone close to her ear.

"Hello Victor." She paused. "Yes, but why are you still in Belgium? I thought you were coming straight home... What sort of trouble? Are you hurt?... Well, when will you be back?... If you don't want to tell me, what am I supposed to do? Well, call me when you are prepared to tell me what's going on." She rang off. "Sorry about that, my husband seems to be in some sort of trouble in Belgium but he says he can't tell me what. To be honest, I'm not too bothered. He's a big boy now; he can look after himself."

On Monday morning, the staff at Viman Developments were bracing themselves for the mayhem that they knew would follow the disclosures of Friday's planning meeting. Their only consolation was that Victor Manning would take all the flack; they merely did as they were told. And they were expecting Manning to park his Jaguar on the forecourt and walk through the door any minute.

The first person through the door was a police detective.

"I'm looking for Mr Manning, is he here?

The young receptionist said nervously, "He's not here at the moment. I'll get his secretary for you."

Angela tried to keep calm as she spoke to the detective. "Mr Manning is on his way back from Belgium. He has been there all weekend motor racing. He assured me on Friday he would be back in the office first thing. We're expecting him any minute."

"In that case, you won't mind if I wait for him. I've already been to his house and didn't find anyone there." He sat down and made himself comfortable.

The telephones were ringing. Staff were frantically printing incoming emails from solicitors representing disgruntled home-owners and housing associations. Still they waited for their employer.

Feeling she was unable to wait any longer, Angela called Manning on his cell phone.

"I'm sorry to call you, Mr Manning, but what time do you expect to be in the office? It really is chaotic here and there's a policeman waiting to talk to you… Oh! I don't understand, and I don't know what to say."

"If that's Manning on the phone I need to talk to him now!" The policeman took the telephone from Angela. "Where exactly are you, Mr Manning? And why have the Belgian police confiscated your passport? We need to talk to you here; there are some very serious accusations being made. We will make an application to our Belgian colleagues and if necessary, travel to Spa to interview you." He turned to Angela, "Well, your boss won't be coming back any time soon."

Angela tried to take control of the situation; she was Manning's secretary and as such, knew how things were run. She wasn't a building technician – there were other people to handle that side of the business – but she was a good organiser. She would do her best to handle things. She gathered all the office staff together.

"It seems Mr Manning has been delayed in Belgium. At the moment I'm not sure when he will be back. In the meantime, we have to handle the current crisis. This is most important: do not under any circumstances discuss anything that goes on in this office with anyone outside the company. No discussions with partners or friends, and definitely no talking to any newspapers. And it goes without saying, no mention on any social media sites. Is that clear?

"Any phone calls, texts, letters or emails from any house owner or housing association, refer them to our solicitors. Do not ever offer any sort of apology, be non-committal to any complaints. Do not say 'I'm sorry to hear that' or words similar; instead, say 'I've heard what you said and I will relay your comments to the appropriate department'. We really need to talk to Mr Harrison. If he contacts any of you, please refer him to me."

TWENTY-NINE

It was early Tuesday morning. Andy had loaded the film set display the night before; now he was on his way to deliver it to the address he had been given. The irony of the situation wasn't lost on him. Not too long ago he was doing a similar task as an employee, now he was doing it as an entrepreneur. He was both nervous and excited at the same time; nervous that he didn't quite know what to expect, excited that this was an insight into a new world. He easily found the location and reported to the office. A young lady introduced herself.

"I'm the second AD. If you drive to the rear of the farmhouse, there will be someone there to help you unload. Our props director is there waiting for you."

Andy didn't know what a second AD was nor did he know what she did, but as instructed, he drove to the rear of the building. He didn't know what a props director did or what they might look like. All these terms were new to him. He quickly found out that the props director was a middle-aged lady dressed in scruffy jeans and a puffer jacket.

"Great, you're here. Let's have a look at these new props."

With that, they opened the van doors and proceeded to unload the furniture and display items.

"Fabulous, these are exactly as Naome described them to me and absolutely perfect for this scene. I can't tell you how pleased I am."

Thinking quickly on his feet, Andy didn't want to let on that this was his first introduction to a film set. He didn't want to appear green or naive.

"When Naome saw them displayed in my shop she told me they were just what you wanted. I'm happy that you feel the same way. She said that you would probably need them for about a month, is that right?"

"Yes, a month is about right. Can we give you a ring when we are finished?"

"Yes, sure."

"Leave your number with the second AD in the office. She's also got our covering order for you. Can I ask, do you supply a lot of props for Naome? Let me explain. She is brilliant at finding hard-to-get items, but as you know, she works as an independent. If we are stuck we ask for her help but she is in such demand that we can't always get hold of her. It would be marvellous to have you as a back-up. Do you have access to this type of period furnishings?"

Still thinking on his feet and beginning to realise the implications of where this conversation might be going, he assured her, "This kind of thing is bread and butter to us. If you can give me a couple of days' notice, I can generally come up with anything, and we have a brilliant designer on our team who can ensure that the various items are all in sync." Andy thought that was probably the right answer. But this was someone who didn't know that a second AD was a second assistant director. "I'll leave my card in the office. You can contact me directly or via Naome. It's been nice to meet you. Do give me a call if I can help."

He collected the order, left his card and started the drive home.

At the shop, Penny had been busy creating a new display. She had found an art deco-style wardrobe, so the new showpiece was a 1930s bedroom, complete with vintage scent bottles and silver-backed hairbrushes on the matching dressing table. An old Lloyd Loom wicker chair and light, flowery, framed watercolours hanging on the wall completed the theme.

When Andy arrived back, Susan had already sold the dressing table.

"Don't take your coat off, Andy. This lady would like the dressing table delivered as soon as you can."

"Right, I'll do that now. Give me the address."

An hour later he was back in the shop.

"Crikey, after just two days we are already feeling the benefit of Penny's presence."

Hundreds of miles away in the small Belgian town of Spa, Victor Manning was sitting in his dated and shabby hotel bedroom. He had spent the morning talking to his office on his cell phone. His once-respected building company was now the focus of media and police attention. Many of his once satisfied and happy customers were now baying for his blood. They had been courted by unscrupulous no win no fee legal vultures who had suggested that they could receive massive compensation for having bought a Viman Developments home. Of course, they were the private buyers who really had little to complain about; the real claims would come from the housing associations who had bought his houses in the hundreds, houses like those in Hollybush Close, and these were the companies that had access to top legal firms, these were the companies that would either cripple Victor Manning or throw him a lifeline.

Manning considered his options. It was obvious that the Belgian authorities were intent on prosecuting him for what they saw as an assault on the barmaid. If he was lucky, he might be found innocent or the charges might be dismissed; on the other hand, what sentence would they impose if he was found guilty? Manning considered that a probable sentence might be a few months. Yeah, he could do that.

He turned his thoughts to the UK police. What charges could they bring? Presumably, they could link him to Jaques and the threats to Andy and Susan. Jaques' sideline of importing counterfeit car parts had nothing to do with him. Sure, he knew about it, but that was all.

As far as he knew, there was no actual law against building inferior houses. No one had died in one of his houses. He could lay the blame for much of the bad practice on his workforce. What sentence could he get for conspiracy to threaten? Maybe a couple of years, reduced to half for good behaviour. Yeah, he could do that.

What about the company? If the lawyers did sue, they could close the business down and take the assets in the bank. He didn't know exactly what was in the bank, but he guessed it wasn't too much, possibly just under a million. If push came to shove, he could lose that. The manor house was in his wife's name, so that was safe. That left his own personal assets.

His UK bank accounts held enough money to ensure he could live comfortably for the rest of his life. His offshore investments were the icing on the cake. Carefully hidden from prying eyes and professionally managed over the past thirty years, they had increased to levels that he could never have imagined. Yes, he knew he was okay for money.

So, planning for the worst, he might serve one or two months in a Belgian jail, possibly followed by a year or so in an open prison in the United Kingdom, and then he would be out. Fair enough, the business might be gone but he had grown tired of it anyway. He would be disgraced by the press, but for how long? After a couple of months everyone would have forgotten about Victor Manning the crooked builder. By then he could be sitting in a beach bar in Spain or Mexico or anywhere he pleased. Suddenly life didn't seem too bad. He decided to accept his fate. He called his solicitor in England.

"I'm in a spot of bother at the moment."

"Yes, we have seen the news items and so, it seems, has everyone else. We've had several claims from housing associations and a few from firms representing private buyers. You will need to give us instructions on how we handle this."

"Well, unfortunately that's not the end of it. I'm stuck in Spa – it's a town in Belgium – and the local police have taken my passport. I'm accused of assaulting a local girl and I'm waiting to go to court. Yes, I know it's a mess. Unfortunately that's not all. The UK police have been on to me about my involvement in threatening a witness against my planning applications. Look, the fact is I could fight these charges and maybe I might get away with it, but I've been doing a lot of thinking and I've come to the decision to throw my hands up to all of it and take what's coming. If I'm lucky, two or three years from now, all this will be behind me and I can retire to the sun. Frankly, I'm fed up with all this ducking and diving. I just want to put it all behind me."

"I understand what you are saying, Victor. For our part we will try to settle all these claims out of court. That should reduce the publicity and be cheaper in the long run. Regarding your present situation, we'll contact one of our colleagues in Belgium and arrange for them to represent you in court and explore any mitigating circumstances. In the meantime, we will stay in regular contact with you and your office. If and when we get any specific claims, we will let you know. At the moment, everyone is shadow boxing with nothing definite on paper."

Manning rang off. He tried to contact Derek Harrison. No answer. He called his wife again.

"Hello Penny. Just be quiet for a few minutes and listen to me. First, I'm absolutely fine but I'm stuck here in Belgium and I've had time to do some serious thinking. I have to tell you, the local police have taken my passport away and I'm waiting to go to court. It's not as bad as it sounds. I was talking to the barmaid at the hotel and things got out of hand. One thing led to another and I just got carried away. I didn't actually touch her but the police claim it was attempted rape, but believe me, it was nothing like that. On top of that, the latest planning application was well and truly rejected and that antiques dealer that I had trouble with before has stirred things up and claimed that many of my houses were built below the required standard. On top of that, he has claimed that I tried to intimidate him and his partner."

"Victor!"

"No, I'm not finished. To be honest, I did try and put the frighteners on him and his girlfriend, who turns out to be Derek's wife, to stop him talking at the planning meeting and, well, it seems the UK police have got involved and they might be coming over here to interview me. That's it."

"That's it! What do you mean, 'that's it'? I thought I was talking to my husband, not some sort of career criminal. What a mess you've got yourself into. And why are you phoning me? What could I do to help even if I wanted to? Which I don't. Before you say another word against them, I'm working with the two antiques dealers you threatened. Like you said, I never intended that to happen, but it did and I've had more fun and enjoyment in the past two days than I can remember. They are two genuine, sincere and friendly people. I enjoy their company and they appreciate my contribution to their business. For once, I know I am making a difference. Victor, I've had enough of you and your dodgy dealings, and as for you threatening people who don't agree with your plans, that is the last straw."

He cut her short. "That's what I've been trying to tell you. Being stuck here in Belgium has given me time to think. I realise now that I have been an idiot. The early years of the business were good, in the beginning we both enjoyed it and the money was good, but it was never enough for me. I always wanted more. And when I couldn't get it or someone got in my way, I made decisions that now I regret. I think I'm going to get plenty of time to reflect on my mistakes."

"What does that mean?"

"Well, the Belgian police are going to charge me with something, possibly assault or maybe attempted rape, I just don't know, and I'm expecting to be charged by the UK police over the intimidation case. Look! Don't say anything, just listen. At the most, I think I might get a custodial sentence for each, possibly two or three years in total. If I'm lucky, that could be reduced to half for good behaviour. I've already decided to be a good boy and take what's coming and when I come out, I'm going to retire to the sun somewhere. Hopefully with you."

"So, what happens to the business?"

"I don't know, I expect it will be wound up by all the lawyers and claims that are coming in thick and fast. Look Penny, I've had enough of the business. I don't care if it folds. From now on, I'm only concerned about me and you."

"For a moment I thought you might have changed, but in your words, you don't care about the business and all those employees who have stuck by you, and you are only concerned about you and me – in that order. Same old Victor Manning. I don't think you have changed, I think you have been caught out by people who will not allow you to bully them. Whether that happens to be a girl in Belgium or my new friends, Andy and Sue. You've been caught and you have decided it might look better for you to say that you are a reformed character. Well, I don't think a leopard can change its spots. Frankly, I don't care about you. At the moment, I'm trying to make my own future." She finished the call with tears rolling down her cheeks.

Susan had heard most of the conversation; it would have been difficult not to in the confined shop.

"Penny, please don't think I was being nosey but I couldn't help overhearing most of what was being said. If you need any time to yourself, just go home, don't worry about us."

"Susan, that's very kind of you but I'd rather be here. I

know I'm making a small contribution and I would rather be here than sitting alone in my empty house."

"It's fine by Andy and me, so long as you are sure. We don't want to say anything that might cause friction between you and your husband. As far as we are concerned, what your husband has done is exactly that, something that *he* has done, not you. You are a totally different person and we welcome your friendship and your contribution to our business."

"Thank you. Now, have you got something in the store room to replace the dressing table that has just been sold?"

Andy heard the question. "I've got one in my lock up back at the flat. It's quite similar to the one that we sold. It does need some work. I'll stay at home tomorrow and get it ready and bring it on Thursday morning."

Penny rearranged the display to compensate for the missing dressing table. She installed a Victorian nursing chair and a small oak coffee table. Neither of them really fitted the design theme but the nursing chair was very nice and quite expensive, whilst the coffee table provided somewhere to display the scent bottle and hairbrushes.

On Wednesday morning, Susan opened the shop whilst Andy stayed in his workshop and prepared the dressing table. Penny joined her a little later. It proved to be a good opportunity for the ladies to discuss their individual feelings on the whole Victor Manning scenario. They were both in similar situations; they had both married men who had allowed themselves to get carried away by greed. Neither of them had been in a position to influence any decisions their partners might have made, and now both of them had fallen out of love with their husbands. And ironically, they had both found a new meaning to their life, one that didn't involve scheming or cheating.

They talked about their own lives, the things they had wanted to happen and the dreams that never materialised.

Susan confided to Penny, "I thought I was happy with Derek. We had a comfortable life. In the early days I enjoyed accompanying him to various award ceremonies and, of course, there were the racing weekends with Victor. But we grew apart. I had this shop, which he financed, but he had no interest in my business, only his own career. Since I met Andy, my life has changed in ways I could never have imagined. I know he is probably instrumental in your husband's downfall, but he is such a genuine and thoughtful person and he has gone through a nightmare with the intimidation and threats from your husband's hired thugs, and he didn't need to do any of it. It was only his desire to help less fortunate people."

Penny listened intently. "I had no idea Victor could do any of the things you are talking about. The slapdash building I can understand, but the violence and threats and the way you were abducted are beyond my comprehension. He was trying to tell me that he is a changed man now, but I doubt it. I would like to believe him but I think it's too late. Su, do you think you might go back to your husband, you know, sometime in the future?"

"No, definitely not. My husband is out of my life for good. Andy and I haven't talked about marriage and obviously there is a big age gap, but I would be so thrilled if I could spend the rest of my life with him. I love him."

The two ladies were quite busy in the shop. This was only the third day Penny had worked there, but her window displays were attracting quite a lot of interest amongst the passing public. A young man bought the antique scent bottle for his girlfriend. He said he was attracted by the shape, so different to anything that you might see in the high street shops of today. While he was in the shop he looked around, as most new customers do, and he was fascinated by an old camera that had been on a shelf for ages. He left with the camera for himself and the scent bottle for his lady. Good business for the shop.

"Penny, I need to run this past Andy but I'm sure he would agree – your presence in the shop is a definite benefit to us and we need to put things on a more business-like basis. Initially we thought that maybe your displays might shift a few bits of old stock, but that order from the film company and the subsequent sales have boosted our takings considerably. When we got home yesterday, Andy and I explored the idea of trying to develop the props hire side of the business. If we did – and it's only an if at the moment – would you be interested in joining us in some kind of partnership?"

"The answer is yes. A definite yes. I've also been thinking and I've got a business plan to offer you. What I would really like to do is set up an interior design and furnishing business, obviously using your knowledge and expertise in sourcing and restoring the items. We could use the shop as a base, but I could also use my house as a showroom – I have several rooms that are not being used at the moment. Prospective customers could look at the furniture as it might look in their own home and we could offer a complete decoration package. I'm able to get good craftsmen through my husband's business. I have a feeling he won't be wanting them now. I actually think many of his men are quite able to work to a top standard but he never gave them the chance. I don't know enough about your business, but I feel sure that you could achieve much higher prices for things if they were sold as part of a design package. Some of the people I know are very well connected and for many of them, money is no stumbling block, provided they get the personal service they demand."

Penny was interrupted by a police officer entering the shop.

"Excuse me, ladies, I'm looking for Mrs Derek Harrison."

"Yes, I'm Susan Harrison. How can I help you?"

"I'm Sergeant John Grove. Mrs Harrison, I'm afraid I have some bad news for you. You might want to sit down."

Susan was a bit shocked. She didn't know what to expect. She pulled up an old stool and sat down.

"I'm sorry to tell you that your husband Derek has been in a car accident and he was pronounced dead at the scene. I'm very sorry."

Susan sat with her head in her arms. There were no tears, only sadness.

"Thank you, sergeant. We were estranged and have been for some time, but it still comes as a shock. Do you have details of how it happened?"

"His car was actually found on Monday. It's taken us until now to locate you. One of your old neighbours told us you ran this shop. The car was found in Sussex. It appears he didn't brake for a corner and ran into a tree. It looks like driver error. The local police conducted a preliminary check of the vehicle and found it to be in good mechanical condition. This was backed up by a garage receipt for a recent service and brake overhaul that they found in the glove box.

So, it appears that the car was properly maintained. We also found a suitcase in the boot. It looked like he was going away somewhere."

"Yes, officer, he was implicated in the planning controversies involving Viman Developments, you've probably read about that in the newspapers. I think it's possible that he was running away. But as I said, we have been separated for some time. I don't really know anything about his day-to-day movements."

"Thank you for your help, Mrs Harrison. We will need to contact you again, and you might need to make the necessary arrangements. If you can, please give me your current address and a contact number."

Susan gave him her phone number and Andy's address, then he left.

Penny broke the silence. "I'll put the kettle on, you just sit quiet for a bit."

"Thank you, Penny, you are kind. Lord knows you've got enough problems of your own. We are both in the same boat regarding our husbands; we've both grown apart from them but neither of us would wish any harm to them. Certainly not death. I know there will be lots of things to sort out, but for the immediate future, I'm going to try to forget what's happened and concentrate on my life as it is now, not what it was in the past."

Susan and Penny sat quietly. They were both lost in their own thoughts. Susan reflected on the life she used to share with her husband. At times it was good, sometimes very good, but the life she now shared with Andy was good all the time.

Penny also thought about the old days, when Victor was starting his business and everything was new and exciting, but she realised that before too long, his desire to make money and the ruthlessness that came with that decision took over his life. She knew that was the point when she started to lose her husband. The long hours and furtive phone calls, and that bloody racing car.

They finished the day lost in their own thoughts.

In the small apartment, Susan told Andy about the death of her husband. She repeated everything Sergeant Grove had told her. She remembered what he had said word for word. In her subconscious mind, she knew that she would always remember the exact time he entered the shop, how he looked, how he smelled and exactly what he said. Andy stayed silent; he knew she had to talk about her husband's death in her own way. His mind went back to the time he realised his own marriage was over. He remembered only too well how he felt and how he blamed himself.

When she was finished he held her by the hand. "Su, he was your husband, you shared your life with him, you loved him and he loved you. I would never try to take those memories away from you. I'm sorry he has gone, but believe me, I will do everything I can to make you happy for the rest of your life. We are a good team together and if you have to deal with the various formalities concerning the accident and his death, you know I will help in any way I can."

"I've said this before, but I'll say it again. Andy Packford, you are one in a million. I love you so much."

"And I love you."

Susan sat quietly for a few minutes, then she started to tell Andy about Penny's suggestion of developing the interior design and furnishing business.

"Su, that sounds like a brilliant idea. We would have to work out some sort of financial arrangements but if we started fairly small and built it up, it could be a perfect move for us into a more lucrative market. If the film props side of things were to develop as well, we could really be getting somewhere. A few weeks ago, I never thought we would be planning a business future with Victor Manning's wife!"

In Spa, Belgium, Victor Manning reported to the police station as usual. On previous occasions, the duty sergeant had produced a book of attendance and Manning had signed it to indicate he had made the required appearance. Today, however, was different. The officer knew him by sight; in fact, everyone at the police station knew him. To them, he was the rich Englishman who had tried it on with a Belgian girl and got caught.

"Ah, Mr Manning, you are to report here tomorrow morning at eight a.m. exactly. Your trial is scheduled to start at nine thirty. We will transport you there."

"Hold on a minute, I haven't spoken to a solicitor yet. I am entitled to a defence barrister."

"Yes, and you will get one, provided free by our legal system. He will meet you in court."

"It doesn't give me much time."

The duty sergeant shrugged his shoulders, "Tomorrow, eight a.m. Don't be late."

Manning returned to his shabby hotel. His watch showed six thirty local time, five thirty in the UK. He called his office. "Angela. Look, I'm due in court tomorrow. I don't know what is going to happen. Between you and me, it looks as if they have already decided I'm guilty. What's happening in the office?"

"Mr Manning, things here are out of control. We've have had several solicitors on the phone, each representing a different housing association, each of them saying the same thing. Basically, they are claiming that the houses their clients bought from Viman are all substantially below standard and that the associations have a responsibility to rehouse their tenants, which will leave them many thousands of pounds out of pocket. Money that they intend to recoup from Viman Developments. The police have been back as well and they have taken away your computer. Frankly, the staff have nothing to do as we don't have any building work ongoing, and they are worried they might not get this month's pay cheque. I'm trying to handle the situation but I'm not sure what's happening or what I'm supposed to do."

"Angela, this is the position: I'm anticipating the Belgian authorities giving me a prison sentence, hopefully a short one, maybe a month or two. When I come out, the UK police are after me for conspiring to intimidate the antiques dealer who tried to scupper our building plans. Yeah, I know it's a mess and now I've had time to reflect on things, I suppose I deserve it all. To be honest, I've resigned myself to accept whatever they throw at me. I can't do much else.

"Look, let's try to get the business as straight as we can. The site workers are already laid off. Get the accountant to make all the office staff redundant and pay them up to date while we still have some money in the bank. Redirect all claims for compensation to the solicitors, let them sort it out. I would like you to stay on in the office to handle whatever correspondence might come in. When I know what is happening, I'll give you a forwarding address so you can send any mail to me. Angela, at the end of all this, I will remember what you have done for me and I will see you right."

"Okay Mr Manning, I understand all that. I can't say anymore at the moment. Good luck!"

She rang off and Manning was left alone with his thoughts in a shabby hotel room in a foreign country.

At eight fifteen on Thursday morning, Victor Manning was sitting handcuffed in the backseat of a police car. Twenty minutes later, he was standing in the dock with a poker-faced policeman either side of him. He confirmed his name when asked in English, and in English he swore on a bible. That was it.

He didn't understand the prosecution counsel and he didn't understand his own barrister, despite a five-minute conversation beforehand in perfect English. He was turned around by his guards and marched out.

Outside the courtroom, he lost his composure. "What happened? Was it adjourned or were the charges dropped? Why didn't they talk to me in English?"

One of the guards smirked. "Because you are in Belgium and you will be staying here for one year. Maybe less if you are lucky, maybe more if you are a naughty boy."

Manning was stunned. His knees buckled and his head was spinning. Telling yourself that you can handle a prison sentence is one thing; the reality of knowing that you will serve it is another. He guessed a twelve-month sentence might mean six months with good behaviour as it did in England, but how did that work in Belgium? What sort of prison would it be? He couldn't cope. His brain wouldn't let him; he had too many questions going through his mind.

He collapsed in a heap, sobbing like a baby. The guards dragged him to his feet and, without giving him any dignity or sympathy, half carried, half marched him into the waiting prison van.

Andy and Susan woke early. They had discussed the possibilities and implications of Penny's business proposal long into the night. They could both see that there were a lot of positives and not many negatives. If the ideas worked, they would all benefit; if they failed, they might have some expensive stock on their hands for a short while, but they knew that eventually they would be able to sell it on.

They drove to the shop to find Penny waiting for them. As they walked through the door, Andy's phone rang.

"Hello. Am I talking to Andy?"

"Yeah. Hello. Who is calling?"

"Andy, my name is Charles. I work with Naome, she's asked me to call you. We desperately need a Victorian sewing work box and, if possible, some genuine sewing implements – is that the right term? You know, scissors, thimbles, that kind of thing. It all needs to be in good condition and it needs to be the right Victorian period. They are going to be used for a close-up shot so they need to be right. Can you help?"

"Yes, we can do that, I have the pieces in stock. When is it needed for and for how long?"

"We need it now, I mean *right now*. It's only for one scene; you could wait and take them back again after the shot. I'll give you the address, it's not far from you. And Andy, you have got us out of a big hole. We really do appreciate it."

Andy rang off.

"Things really are looking up! That was one of Naome's men after a sewing box. He said I can wait and bring it back after the shoot. This is better than selling the things."

He loaded the van and set off. This time he knew the drill. When he got to the address, he looked for the AD's office and announced himself. The AD directed him to the set and, as on the previous location, he was met by the property director who took charge of the props.

"Well done, this is exactly what we wanted. We had tried to use some modern bits; they looked okay to the naked eye but they looked awful through the camera. This scene will probably take about two hours. Do you want to grab a coffee while you wait?"

So, he grabbed a coffee and waited. This was a completely new world to Andy but he was learning fast. He sensed that if you could provide the goods and you were prepared to put yourself out, there was money to be made. Lots of money.

Two hours came and went. After three and a half hours they called a wrap, which Andy guessed meant the film shoot was over. He collected his pieces and loaded them back into the van. He caught the property director as she was leaving the set.

"Has the AD got my official order?"

"No. Look, this was all done on the spur of the moment. I'll go with you to the AD. I think we'll pay you cash, that's easier, isn't it?"

"Yes, that's fine by me."

The props director and the AD held a short, mumbled discussion before reaching what seemed like an agreement. The AD counted out four hundred pounds and asked Andy to sign a receipt.

"I hope that's okay for you."

Andy tried to look casual, as if this kind of thing was a normal business transaction for him. Always quick on his feet and not wanting to sound like a beginner, Andy replied, "Yes that's fine. I actually had it costed out at four twenty, but four hundred is okay. Thank you."

Four hundred, is that okay! Andy would have sold the lot and delivered it for half that amount.

On the drive back to his shop, Andy's thoughts were full of the possibilities that this new business venture might offer. He was well aware that there would be a few bridges to cross and probably a few changes to be made. But as he saw things, he and Susan were more than able to source whatever the film people might need. If they didn't have it in stock, they could find it at one of a dozen local auctions.

They would concentrate on maintaining enough good quality stock and leave Penny to design eye-catching window displays, something that they knew she could do brilliantly. Penny could also run the interior design business, which would run hand and glove with the window displays. Susan would run the shop while he managed and expanded the prop hire side of things.

He had it all mapped out in his mind. He even had a new name for the fledgeling business: Packford Harrison Manning. PHM Production Properties.

Inside the van, Manning sat in silence. The two other prisoners spoke in French. He couldn't understand what they were saying so he had no way of knowing whether they were talking about him or to him, but the occasional glance in his direction led him to believe that somehow he featured in their discussion. He knew that now was the time he would have to make a decision if he was to survive for the next twelve months. He could knuckle under, become a perfect prisoner and hope that the guards and the other inmates would see him for what he was and leave him alone. After all, he was not exactly a master criminal. He was someone who fancied his chances with a girl who did not want to play. Wrong girl, wrong day. Every man has been there.

Or he could tough it out, make sure from day one that no one pushed him around. He couldn't let these two in the van tell their mates how the stupid Englishman had been the victim of their jokes without him even knowing it.

He chose to tough it out.

"Oi! You two! If you've got something to say to me, say it so I can hear it and understand it, otherwise keep your comments to yourselves. You can all speak bloody English when you want to. I've been stitched up by my own lawyer. I don't need to put up with the likes of you having a laugh at my expense."

"Okay, English. Take it easy. We were just saying, one year inside for touching her tits. Don't your English girls have tits?" They both laughed. Manning forced a laugh.

"Yeah, English girls have tits and they don't cry rape if you touch them. I guess I've learned my lesson. Only English girls for me from now on. My name's Vic, what do I call you?"

"They call me Nico and my friend is called Ed. You know what, English, we weren't sure but you are alright."

Manning smiled inwardly. He had won the first battle.

The gates opened and the prison van drove through into a courtyard. A guard opened the van doors. Manning stepped out, followed by the others. They were ushered through a security door into the processing area. Any valuables they had were taken and logged, then they were stripped, escorted into the shower and finally given prison-regulation tracksuits.

They were marched in single file, Manning sandwiched between the other two, a prison guard front and rear. No one spoke.

The first thing to hit Manning was the noise, the second was the smell. The noise reminded him of a football match, the smell, of a public toilet after a football match.

The guard stopped and they turned. Each of the prisoners faced a cell door, which was opened remotely by another guard at the end of the corridor. The guards gently but forcefully pushed them into their respective cells. The doors closed behind them.

When Andy got back to the shop, the ladies were waiting. Susan asked, "Well, how did it go? Did they use the work box?"

"They certainly did and we got paid cash. There's no doubt there is a lot of money in the filming business."

Susan was quick to reply. "You're not the only one to be busy. We've had a good afternoon here, haven't we, Penny?"

"Okay, you heard my news, what have you girls got to tell me?"

Penny continued the conversation. "A friend of mine heard that I was working in your antiques shop and she called by today to ask if we could furnish her new conservatory, which is currently being built. She wants a classical eighteenth-century French look. Frankly, I didn't have a clue. I wouldn't know eighteenth-century French from the twentieth century, but thanks to Susan, we managed to sit down together and make some designs and get some idea of cost. My friend was very impressed. We can't really do much more until the building work is completed, then it will be a case of detailed planning and giving her a final costing. I know the lady well and I know the circles she mixes in; this could be a brilliant start for us."

Andy looked at Susan and Penny. "Come on girls, let's have a group hug. Our future together is beginning to look very good!"

The next two weeks were hectic in the antiques shop. Penny's window displays were creating a steady flow of new customers, which had a knock-on effect for the other local shops. Whenever Andy or Su called into the newsagent next door, he would tell them that his sales had increased significantly thanks to the extra passing trade. The nearby café had also benefitted from increased trade. The irony of the situation wasn't lost on Andy. He might have contributed to the downfall of a building company, but he was something of a saviour to the local shops.

Although the extra sales were good for their shop, Andy and Susan knew they would have to work harder to maintain their stock of good quality antiques. This would mean travelling further to auction houses and being particularly careful to select only the best or most appropriate items. Andy was quite happy to accept that challenge. He knew Susan was more than capable of running the shop on her own, leaving Penny free to work on her window displays and to act as a designer and negotiator for the interior design work. He knew the intimidation from Manning's thugs was a thing of the past and consigned to history, but the realisation that Susan's terror had been caused by his actions still weighed heavily on his mind. He was determined that he would never again do anything that might put her in danger.

Over the past weeks, the police had kept Susan informed of the formalities regarding her husband's death. She realised that at some stage there would need to be a coroner's inquest before a formal death certificate could be issued and a funeral arranged. When she eventually received the notification, it still came as a shock and reminded her of her current situation.

She was a widow in her forties living with her boyfriend, nearly twenty years her junior. She had no family, no savings, no property of her own; everything that she owned and loved was in the shop, literally. Expressed in those terms, it was scary, yet she had never been so happy. The future scared and excited her in equal measures. But now she must face the coroner's court before she could move on.

Susan and Andy entered the courtroom together. For Susan it was a new and frightening experience. Although Andy had previously attended the hearing into the deaths of the Jones family and knew how the process worked, it was still an intimidating building. As they took their seats, Andy looked around and recognised a familiar face in the row behind.

"How are you, Jack? How are things at our favourite local newspaper?"

"Oh, pretty good thanks, Andy. You certainly stirred up a hornet's nest when you got involved with Manning and his activities. Mind you, I'm not complaining; the paper has sold a few more copies thanks to you. I take it you have heard the latest news on Manning? He was found guilty of sexually assaulting a girl in Belgium and they gave him twelve months inside. Between you and me, I've got a feeling we won't be hearing much more about him. Victor Manning's days as a local high-flyer are over. And that is thanks to you."

"Jack, Susan and I just want to get through today and start putting all this behind us. We're moving on quickly with the business and recently we've made some very significant contacts that hopefully will pay big dividends for us."

"I'm pleased to hear it. You've both had a hard time lately, you deserve a bit of good luck."

The coroner opened the inquiry by outlining the facts.

"Derek Harrison was found dead inside his crashed car. The police report stated that his car was travelling at high speed. Several witnesses told police that they had been overtaken by his vehicle, which in their opinion was being driven too fast for the road conditions.

"The police examination of the crash scene indicated that he failed to slow down for a corner and consequently, he crashed into a roadside tree. As a result, he sustained severe head injuries that proved fatal. The police report also found that he was not wearing a seatbelt. There was no evidence that he had been drinking. Further investigation of his car revealed that it had recently been serviced and the brake pads had been replaced. However, although the brake parts looked new, they appeared to be of very inferior quality as the pads had worn down to a level that rendered them useless. Under normal conditions, the parts concerned might be expected to last several thousands of miles; however, it appeared these particular examples had only lasted a handful of miles. These are the facts of the case. It is my duty to establish a cause of death. I find that the deceased Derek Harrison died due to misadventure. His excessive speed contributed to his death, which in my opinion was caused by the ineffective brake components fitted to his car. I am recommending that the police investigate further to establish who supplied and fitted these substandard parts, and if a criminal act was committed, that the appropriate action be taken."

Considering the circumstances, Susan remained remarkably composed. The coroner's verdict did not tarnish her husband's name or reputation, other than by the fact that he had elected not to wear a seatbelt. She was happy that for the time being at least, he still had his good name. Whatever problems there might have been within their marriage, they would stay a secret from those it didn't concern.

Andy realised that the coroner's comments regarding the substandard brake parts were directly related to the evidence he and Harry Thornton had found at Jeremy Jaques' warehouse. He knew that the police were already investigating Jaques' criminal activities and that in due course there would be a police prosecution, and inevitably he and Harry would be called as witnesses. But that was for some time in the future. For now, he would need to stand by Susan and support her through the coming weeks. The inquest was the start of her ordeals; next would be her husband's funeral, followed by the process of settling his estate, reading and administering his will.

Andy was aware of the strain this would put on Susan. But he knew she was a strong woman, a woman who knew her own mind and a woman who was determined to live her life the way she wanted.

The next few days proved to be stressful for Susan and difficult for Andy. The business was flourishing; many more customers through the door kept the finances on a stable footing. Although it was too early to expect any financial reward for their interior design work, it was only a matter of time before one of their schemes was accepted and completed. Susan tried to carry on as normal, concentrating all her efforts into the business and pushing the thoughts of her late husband's funeral and finalising his affairs to the back of her mind. Andy was spending more and more time away from the shop; he was either sourcing new stock or he was delivering the larger items customers had bought. This was on top of the demands made by the film studios.

That original request from Naome had started a very large ball rolling. At the time, Andy thought it was just a one-off lucky break. He didn't know how the industry worked and he had no idea of the volume of work that he might receive. He quickly realised that although the film industry was massive, it was also a very close-knit community. It didn't take him long to understand that if he established a name for himself as a supplier of authentic props, and if he was prepared to jump to their command, there would be no limit to the amount of orders he might receive. The work was interesting and the cost seemed irrelevant, but for Andy it came at a price. Tomorrow was no good, everything had to be *now*, immediately. Sometimes it could be done but sometimes it couldn't. If they were to succeed in this new business, they would need a bigger inventory of stock and somewhere to store it all. Suddenly a laid-back, easygoing antiques shop was thrust into a new hectic, demanding environment.

THIRTY

The day that Susan was dreading arrived too quickly. She had planned that the funeral would be a quiet affair. The marriage hadn't produced any children, her husband had been an only child, his parents had died many years before, so there wouldn't be many people at the service. A quiet affair.

Andy parked his old BMW in the crematorium car park. He and Susan walked from the car park to the small chapel. He held her hand as they walked with their heads bowed. They didn't look left or right. Why would they? He was there to support his partner. He knew the marriage was over before he met her but he blamed himself for the position they now found themselves in. As they walked, Andy's thoughts went back to the first conversation they had had together. It had not been so long ago, but so much had happened to both of them since then. Much of it had been good, but he was aware that his intervention in Victor Manning's building plans had contributed to her husband's death. He knew it and he knew that Susan knew it.

The chapel was virtually empty. Andy noticed Mark Seymour sitting in the back row. Near to him was the reporter from the local newspaper. There were a small handful of other mourners. Andy guessed they might have been work mates or neighbours. He acknowledged them with a small nod of his head as he and Susan took their seats at the front.

It was a bland, humanist service. A few words about celebrating Derek Harrison's life, all very sterile. And it was over. Not much to mark the passing of a human being, but then again, maybe he didn't deserve any more. His complacency had contributed to the deaths of three totally innocent people; it had also caused misery for countless tenants in awful houses that he had allowed Victor Manning to build.

The small group of mourners followed Susan and Andy out of the chapel, heads bowed, walking slowly. No one spoke. Outside the sun was shining as they gathered in a small group. Mark Seymour was the first to speak.

"I'm sorry about your husband, Mrs Harrison. I never knew him that well, but we worked together on many of Viman's developments. I know he was under a lot of pressure from Manning and I think he allowed himself to be intimidated by him. To be honest, I think everybody who worked with Victor Manning was intimidated in one way or another. It wasn't easy to say no to him. The firm has all but collapsed now. Angela is staying on for the moment just to handle any mail, but the rest of us are out of a job. At the moment I'm looking but there isn't much out there. I'm hoping something might turn up soon."

Susan only knew Seymour by association. She had heard Derek talk about him and more recently Andy had mentioned him in conversations.

"Thank you, Mark, for coming, I suppose it's nice for people that he worked with to come to his funeral. To be honest, I just want to put all this behind me now. Derek and I haven't been close for a long while and all the business between Andy and your old boss has had a massive effect on me. I just want to move on. I don't know if you have heard, but Penny Manning is working with us and we have some new and exciting things happening to our antiques business that we are concentrating on at the moment. It's ironic, isn't it? Victor Manning tried to crush us but his wife is proving to be our saviour."

Andy turned to Seymour. "Mark, don't build your hopes up, but if you are still looking for a job in a month or so, call into the shop. We might – and I only said might – have something for you. We could be looking for a project manager for our new interior design business."

"Thank you. If nothing else materialises, I'll definitely get in touch. I really do appreciate you thinking of me."

Mark Seymour bid them goodbye and walked back to his car. Andy turned to Jack and joked, "We need to stop meeting like this, people will start talking."

"Andy, they are already talking. You are beginning to get a reputation around here. First it was exposing Manning and his dirty tricks, then it was Jeremy Jaques and his strong-arm men, not to mention his counterfeit car spares. You're a regular hero to a lot of folks. Now I hear you're moving into the movie business. Is there no stopping you?"

"Shush! It's not meant to be common knowledge. I don't want every Tom, Dick and Harry jumping on the bandwagon. But yes, we have made some good contacts in the industry and they are using some of our stock as props in their films. Jack, that's off the record, don't go writing a story about it."

"Fair enough, Andy. I've already had some good copy from you, so mum's the word."

Susan and Andy started to walk back to their parked car. The pathway to the car park curved gently through a decorative garden area with rustic wooden benches either side. They took no notice of the elegantly dressed man sitting on his own. As they passed, he rose to his feet and followed a few yards behind. Before they had a chance to get into Andy's car, the man interrupted them.

"Mrs Harrison, can I have a word with you, please? I could have spoken to you earlier but I wanted to make sure your husband was really dead."

"I beg your pardon? Who the devil are you and what has my husband's death got to do with you?"

"You see, your late husband and I had a business deal going on. To put it simply, in exchange for a consideration, he made sure that any plans I submitted were passed by the council. I assume he had a similar arrangement with Manning; in fact, I think he had the same arrangement with several builders. You see, it worked like this – every year I bought him an expensive new car and in exchange, he made sure I would get my building plans passed. Well, the problem is he crashed his new car before he passed my plans, so in a nutshell, I'd like the money, please, for the car – a shade short of thirty-five thousand pounds."

Andy opened the car door.

"Susan, take no notice of him. Just get into the car."

He turned and walked the few paces back to the smartly dressed man.

"I get your point. Let's move away a bit out of earshot and see if we can't sort something out."

Andy gently rested his hand on the man's shoulder and guided him back to the bench where he had been sitting a few minutes earlier. As they sat down, Andy turned slightly so they faced each other, with his back towards the car. He casually placed his right hand along the back of the bench.

"How long have you had this arrangement with Derek Harrison?"

"Several years. It was an open secret that he could be bought. Manning started it, but I think most of the local builders soon cottoned on. Rumour has it some of them gave him a crate of whisky every couple of weeks, but my deal was a new car every year. For me it was a good deal; I could book the car down to my own company, the taxman never asked who actually drove it and the benefits were… well, let's say I could build pretty much whatever I wanted."

Andy smiled. "Sounds easy and I suppose if Manning started it and you carried on, it's a bit like a slice off cut cake."

"Yeah, that's it. He was very co-operative, if you get my meaning. There was one occasion when I had to remind him of his arrangement with Manning. When he realised that it was common knowledge, he was happy to look after me as well. It's not like it was hurting anybody. I'm sure he has taken good care of his wife and, let's face it, the insurance will pay out on the car, so I just want what is mine, a shade under thirty-five grand." He allowed himself a slight smirk.

Andy sat in silence. He tried to stay calm but it wasn't easy. After what seemed like minutes but was probably no more than seconds, he moved closer to the man. Their faces were barely inches apart. He spoke very quietly in a controlled, measured voice.

"Whatever arrangement you had with Susan's husband ended when his car hit that tree. At this moment, she is sitting in my car reflecting on her life with her late husband. When I get back to her, she'll probably ask what all this is about and I'm going to tell her it was all a big mistake and you were actually some scammer who thought he would try to bluff his way through it and make some easy money. That is right, isn't it? This is just a scam? Because if you are planning anything that might destroy her happiness, I will make sure that you live to regret your actions. If that is not plain enough, we can settle it here and now, but I'm telling you, you will end up in hospital alongside some of Manning's hired thugs. This finishes right here, right now. Your choice."

"Well, you talk the talk alright, but you don't scare me. I want my money."

"Andy. There you are, I've been looking for you. I saw Susan sitting in the car. She said you were over here talking to some stranger about a car or something. Frankly, she was a bit too upset to understand what was going on. I've actually been standing behind a bush for ages listening to you and your friend. You know, the thing is with being a newspaper reporter, you are always looking for the next big story, you can never afford to let your guard down. You never know where it might come from. It could be on the street or in a supermarket or even on a bench in a crematorium. I'm glad I had my recorder with me."

"Hi Jack. I think we're done here. My new friend is just going. He got a bit confused and thought I was someone else. I think he realises his mistake now."

The well-dressed man stood up and walked away.

"Thanks Jack, you saved me some more agro there. Do you really have it on tape?"

"Of course I did. I'm a reporter, aren't I? I'll keep it for security, but you'll have to buy the drinks before I edit out your hospital remarks. I might actually write an article about corruption in the building trade. No names, no pack drill, it might just help to clean things up a bit."

Susan didn't feel the need to hold a wake for her late husband. Everyone knew that the spark of love had gone and although they had enjoyed happy times, they were years ago. Her new life was with Andrew Packford, it would have been hypocritical to pretend otherwise. So, they drove back to their apartment so she could remember the good times in peace.

Andy opened the apartment door and stepped over the post that was lying on the mat. Once inside, they changed into more comfortable, casual clothes. Susan made some coffee while Andy opened the day's post.

"Anything interesting?" Susan asked.

"There's a letter for you. It looks like it's from a firm of solicitors. Everything else is junk mail."

Susan opened the letter. "Yes, it's from a firm of solicitors handling Derek's estate. They are asking me to attend the reading of his will. I hadn't really thought about his will. I know he had one, we both did, but I hadn't given it any more thought. They want me to go tomorrow afternoon. I don't really know what to expect. Will you come with me for moral support?"

"Of course I will. You don't need to ask."

Susan was surprised to find the solicitor's office was not all as she was expecting. She had conjured up an image in her head of a traditional oak-panelled office with piles of papers on an old desk and a stereotypical older gentleman looking over half-framed glasses. Instead, she and Andy were ushered into a modern state-of-the-art office with no old files, only computer screens, and a frighteningly young solicitor sitting on a leather Chesterfield sofa. Sitting in a corner of the office was an attractive young girl. Neither Andy nor Susan gave her much notice, only a quick nod and half smile of acknowledgement. The solicitor introduced himself and the young girl, who he called Sofie. He went on to outline the work his practice had undertaken to finalise the estate of Susan's late husband.

"As you may know, we have been acting on your late husband's behalf for some time. We drew up the current will for him and on his written instructions, we have acted as executors and liquidated his property. His instructions were that everything he owned was to be sold to provide a lump sum for his beneficiaries. There are only two, Mrs Harrison and his Daughter Sofie."

As he spoke, he looked and pointed in the direction of the young lady. Sofie turned to look away, trying to avoid Susan's quizzical stare.

Susan didn't know what to say. For seconds, she just sat there. Her brain was racing through the possible explanations. Was Sofie part of another scam? How many more crooks would come out of the woodwork? She couldn't possibly be his daughter, could she?

The solicitor broke the silence.

"This must come as a shock to you, Mrs Harrison. I assume that you didn't know your husband had a daughter with another partner."

Susan couldn't contain herself anymore. She broke down in uncontrollable tears. Her whole body shook with the emotion. Andy took her in his arms and he held her tightly, trying to support her collapsing, shaking body. He spoke to her quietly and slowly.

"Try to stay calm, darling, and we'll sort this out."

"Andy, I've been threatened and kidnapped, my husband has been killed in a car crash. I've found out that he was dishonest, and now I'm being told that he has fathered a child, which, by the way it looks, must have been around the time we got married. I can't take anymore. I really can't."

Andy turned to the solicitor. "As you can see, Susan is very upset with this revelation, she really had no idea. We have both been through some very stressful and difficult times lately. Whilst Susan gets over this latest shock, can you please briefly outline the position we are in at the moment?"

The solicitor glanced across to Sofie. "Are you happy for me to discuss your personal details with Mrs Harrison and Mr Packford?"

"Yes, please do. I have nothing to hide."

"Well, Mrs Harrison and Mr Packford, the late Mr Harrison had a brief relationship with Sofie's mother, who at that time was working as his secretary. This was approximately twenty-one years ago. As a result Sofie was born, and her mother moved away to the south coast to look after her daughter. Mr Harrison kept in contact and over the years he made quite substantial financial contributions to them. Unfortunately, Sofie's mother died three years ago, leaving Sofie, then aged eighteen, to look after herself. Which, I feel compelled to say, she did very well. She now owns her own small café and has a good business. On your late husband's instructions, we have over the years acted as an intermediary between father and daughter. With regards to the position we are in now, we have liquidated your late husband's estate as was his instructions. The total sum of the estate is £512,278.89. There are only two beneficiaries: Sofie Harrison and Mrs Susan Harrison. His wishes were that Sofie should receive 90% and Mrs Harrison 10%. This equates to £461,051 for Sofie and £51,227.89 for you, Mrs Harrison. I have the cheques here and would be very happy to hand them over. I also have a letter for you, Mrs Harrison. I believe it was your husband's intention to start a new life to be near Sofie, and he asked me to give it to you when he was settled there. Obviously, the tragic accident changed things somewhat."

Susan, still crying, looked across to Sofie. "I would like it if we could be friends," she said.

Sofie rose from her seat and walked over to Su, putting her arms around her. She said, "I would like that. I would like it if we could stay in touch. I know my father betrayed you but after my mother died, he did everything possible to help me stand on my own feet, including buying the café for me. Even though he was married to you, he was a real father to me. After Mum died, he often talked about you and in the past year or so, he told me how he regretted that the two of you had drifted apart. Believe it or not, he even told me that he was happy that you had found your own happiness with Andy. Please, let's exchange addresses and promise that we'll keep in touch."

Susan did her best to hold back her tears. Despite the shock, she quickly realised that she liked Sofie and yes, she would like to get to know her better and be part of her life.

Maybe in time, Sofie might be the daughter she had longed for but never had.

The solicitor's relief was plain to see. He had expected a confrontational meeting but instead of aggression and anger, there were smiles and hugs.

Susan took the cheque and the unopened letter from him and started to leave. As her hand went to the door handle, Sofie caught hold of her shoulder.

"Susan and Andy, there is a hotel just down the street – I actually stayed there last night, it's quite nice. Can we just sit there and talk, all three of us? I mean, do you have the time? We don't know anything about each other. I don't want to go back home and miss the opportunity of getting to know you both."

Susan glanced across to Andy with the look between two people that says, 'What do you think?' Andy smiled, first at Susan, then at Sofie.

"Thank you, that would be really nice. We do have a lot to talk about."

The hotel lounge was old but well furnished. They sat around a small coffee table and ordered drinks. Susan started the conversation off.

"You live on the south coast, do you, Sofie? I've always wanted to live by the sea."

"Yes, my mother moved there after… well, you know what I mean. She moved there when I was born. I've lived there ever since. When I left school, I worked in a café. After a few years the owner retired and I got the chance to buy it. As I said before, my father… erm, your husband… offered to buy it for me. I've made quite a few changes. Initially it was a bit of a greasy spoon type of place. I've upgraded it and now we still get workmen after a fry-up breakfast, but later in the day we get young mums and older ladies out for a coffee. Despite how it sounds, the different customers complement each other and we all get along quite well. Tell me what you do. My father said something about antiques."

Susan smiled. "Yes, we both seem to have shops in common. Yours is a café, ours is an antiques shop. I've had the shop for a number of years and, like you, Derek helped me set up. No, that's not fair, he didn't help me set up, he paid for everything and put money in my bank account. I think he might have done it to get me out of his hair, but in fairness I owe him everything. In the early days of our marriage, things seemed to be fine. Obviously, I didn't know anything about your mother and my husband. I don't know if it was an impulse thing or a full-on affair; until half an hour ago, I didn't know anything. But over the years we drifted apart and towards the end there was no love at all. That's when I met Andy. We crossed paths at the antique auctions where technically we were competitors, we were both bidding for the same things, so we joined forces, so to speak. Now we have a thriving shop and also a growing side-line of supplying film props, and we have also recently started an interior design and furnishing business. Unfortunately, there was also a sinister side to your father. He was mixed up with a ruthless property developer who was building dangerous houses that Derek was authorising. Unknowingly, Andy got mixed up with the whole affair, which nearly ended badly for us. But we are past all that now and I have a new... what shall I call you? You're not a step-daughter, you're a..."

"Couldn't I be just a new friend?"

"Of course, I hope you'll be a very dear friend."

With tears rolling down their cheeks, they made their final farewells and went their own ways. When they arrived back at the apartment, Susan collapsed, exhausted, in a chair. "What a day! I didn't know what to expect but I certainly didn't think it would be like this. Sofie seemed such a nice, level-headed young woman. I'm glad that Derek left her most of his money. Now you and I are together, I have everything I ever wanted: a loving relationship, a business that I can be proud of and a future to look forward to. And with the money from Derek's will, a little nest egg behind us. Oh, Andy, I'm so happy."

"Su, you know I feel the same. Hopefully all the stuff with Manning is behind us and we can concentrate on our own lives and futures. I don't think either of us knew what the future might hold but this has to be as good as it gets. Do you want to open the letter the solicitor gave you?"

"Yes. If I open it now, everything is done and finished and we can make a new start tomorrow."

Su took the letter from her handbag and slowly opened it. It was handwritten in the elegant style that she recognised. The style of an artistic person. The style of her late husband, the chief planning officer. Her first thought was to read it to herself but she reconsidered and decided to read it aloud so Andy could hear.

"Andy, I don't want any secrets between us. Whatever my husband wanted to say to me, I want you to hear."

Andy was very quiet and thoughtful. "Look, Su, I'm happy to listen but you don't have to do this. Whatever happened between you and your husband is your business. Don't forget it might not be possible for me to erase something I don't want to hear."

"Andy, I'm prepared to take that chance." She started. "My dearest Susan. I have asked my solicitors to pass this letter to you, I just couldn't do it myself. When you read this, I will be a long way from you.

"As you know, my actions have put me in a very difficult position and as I write this I am preparing to leave the area for good. I don't think we will meet again. If I could turn back time and start again, I would, but of course I can't. When we first met all those years ago, I had lots of ideas. Ideas that I thought would benefit everybody. New, well-designed houses for families to live in. Whole new estates surrounded by green fields with playing areas for children. Homes where people could live and thrive and be proud of, and a rosy future for you and me, but as we all know it didn't turn out like that, did it?

"I really did love you. I still do but I know I'm weak and I let myself be distracted and manipulated. I knew it was happening but I was powerless to stop it. I liked the attention others gave me and by the time I realised I was being taken for a fool, it was too late.

"My first mistake. Oh Susan, I'm so sorry. I allowed myself to be flattered by the attentions of my secretary. I didn't intend things to get that far but I am ashamed to say she had my child. A little girl, Sofie – she is twenty-one now. Three years ago, Sofie's mother died and since then, I've helped her start her own business, a café. In fact, while she was growing up I helped out financially, which brings me to my next mistake.

"The stories you have heard about me and Victor Manning are all true. In fact, it started when Manning found out about my secretary and the baby. He held it over my head so I would turn a blind eye to his dubious building plans. As things went further, he bribed me with money that I needed to send to Sofie's mother. Of course, the news got around that I could be bribed – 'bought', I think is the expression they use – and every builder and developer within a hundred miles jumped on the bandwagon. As often happens, one mistake leads to another and another and before you know what has happened, it's too late to turn back. I was proud of some of the buildings I sanctioned, but others were complete disasters. Obviously, the worst was that dreadful Hollybush Close and that poor family who died as a result of my failures. I will bear the burden of that until the day I die. Although I cursed him at the time, with reflection, I am so pleased that your new partner Andy stood up to Manning and managed to do what I couldn't. I know that you have found an honourable and caring man. I hope you are able to share a long and happy life with him. I'm not sure what I'm going to do. I know I can't stay here. I think I might go to the south coast and be near my daughter. Please take comfort in the fact that in my own way, I will always love you, and I genuinely hope that you find the happiness you deserve. All my love, Derek."

She folded the letter and held it close to her chest. Andy had watched her in silence. He had seen her facial expression change as she read and now tears were slowly rolling down her cheeks.

"Are you okay, Su?"

"Yes, I'm fine, it's just… well, it's a shock. We did drift apart but I think in our own way we still loved each other. Does that make sense?"

Andy thought about his own broken marriage and the regrets he still harboured.

"Of course it makes sense. Love between two people doesn't die; it might change but it doesn't die. I can't forget the good times I shared with my wife and I wouldn't want you to forget the life you shared with your husband. But if you'll let me, I promise I will love you with all my heart for the rest of my life."

"Stop it, Andy! I've already got tears in my eyes, much more and you'll have me bawling like a kid. You must know by now that I'm crazy in love with you. I can't wait to spend the rest of my life with you."

They didn't say much that evening. They sat in the small apartment with their own thoughts. Later, as they lay in bed together, Susan turned to Andy.

"Do you really think all the trouble and stress of recent months is behind us now? Can we settle down with our own lives and not worry about Victor Manning? Is there anything else that might come back to haunt us?"

Andy took her in his arms and held her close to his chest.

"My sweet Su, there might be court cases regarding his thugs and I might have to give evidence, but it's no big deal. After what we have already been through, we can handle anything. Trust me."

She fell asleep in his arms. Tomorrow would be another day.

In the back room of the shop, Andy answered the telephone.

"Hello, Jack. How are you? We haven't spoken since the day of Susan's husband's funeral. And that was nearly a year ago. How's my favourite newspaper reporter doing? Any scoops lately?"

"No scoops, not since you stopped being a superhero crime fighter. But you and Susan are newsworthy again, in a nice way. What I have in mind would make a brilliant story for our readers and it might do you both some good. Can I pop round and run it past you?"

"Yeah, sure. I'm intrigued. See you later."

"Susan, you remember Jack, the reporter at the local newspaper? Well, he's on his way here with a story that he thinks we'll like. I can't wait to hear what he's got."

An hour later, Jack walked through the door of the shop.

"Things have changed around here, haven't they? I see you've taken over the unit next door. Things look very impressive. Which is why I'm here."

"Hello Jack, nice to see you. Is this going to be a business meeting? Do I need to get Susan or are you trying to sell some advertising space?"

"You cheeky sod. I'm here to do you a big favour."

"I guessed as much, Jack, by your phone call. I'm only having a laugh at your expense. Come through to the back and find a seat. I'll get Su. I think she's next door."

The three of them sat down. Jack opened the conversation.

"The last time I talked to you was about a year ago. At that time you were just getting started renting out your antiques as props for the movie business. From what we've heard at the paper, you've got your fingers in other pies as well now. We heard on the grapevine that not only are you now in the interior design business, but that one of your contracts is to be featured on the television programme Dream Homes. This could be a big story for the paper and it won't do you any harm. You can see the headline. 'People's rights campaigner gets top billing on television programme.' Are you both with me? Do you see the upside of this?"

"We see where you are coming from, Jack. We didn't know anything about the TV programme; obviously our client contacted them herself. Before we go any further, it's only right that we get Penny Manning and our contracts manager Mark Seymour to join us. They are the two people who plan and run that side of our business." Andy called them both in and made the introductions to Jack. He carried on, "Mark, Penny, did you know that one of our schemes is to be featured on Dream Homes?"

Mark gave a smug smile. "I think that must be Mrs Atkinson. I know she was very happy with the work we did for her, both Penny's design and the quality of the finished job. At the time she was telling all her friends about it and we've actually had a couple of new jobs on the back of it. When I inspected the finished job with her, she wanted to give me a tip – which I graciously refused, of course. She is a very influential lady, being married to an MP, so it would be fitting that she would get onto the TV people."

Penny added, "She had some very special demands, most of which we could accommodate; for others, we managed to steer her in a slightly different direction. Like Mark said, I knew she was happy with the finished result. In fact, all our clients are happy, otherwise we wouldn't be getting their work."

Susan turned to the reporter, "I don't know how you propose to cover this, Jack, but presumably you must wait until the programme is shown. I know Andy might be the 'people's campaigner', as you put it, but we are very much a team here. Every member of the team is equally important and we each have a unique quality and a reason to be here. Many of our tradesmen originally worked for Victor Manning, as did Mark. Under Manning's rule, they had no choice but to do as he said; now they can flourish and be proud of the excellent work they produce. Penny was married to Manning and, just like his employees, her talent was unrecognised and her spirit stifled. Me, I'm just a lady who likes antiques. Andy is the one person who pulled us all together and had faith in our ability to do the right thing."

ABOUT THE AUTHOR

I was born in north London just as WW2 ended. I left school at fifteen without any qualifications. I still don't have any. My wife and I moved to Hertfordshire when we married, and more recently to Leicestershire to be near our son and his family. From an early age, I chose to work for myself in several different professions. I have too many interests to list them here but over the years cycling, motorbiking and rock climbing have taken up most of my time.

 Matador

For exclusive discounts on Matador titles,
sign up to our occasional newsletter at
troubador.co.uk/bookshop